"You better say no loud and clear, and say it fast, Rebecca,"

Shane said huskily. "Tell me you don't want me, don't want this. And make damn sure you mean it."

She was melting against him, soft fragrant wax. His blood pumped in response to those soft, sexy sounds she made in her throat.

Under her palm, Rebecca felt the furious beat of his heart, and her hand trembled. She'd thought it was fear, but it wasn't. Oh, no, it wasn't fear. It was longing.

"I can't." She let out a whoosh of breath. "I wouldn't mean it."

Triumph suited him. "I know."

RITA
–Award–
Winning
Author

Dear Reader,

Spring is just beginning in the month of April for Special Edition!

Award-winning author Laurie Paige presents our THAT'S MY BABY! title for the month, *Molly Darling*. Take one ranching single dad, a proper schoolteacher and an irresistible baby girl, and romance is sure to follow. Don't miss this wonderful story that is sure to melt your heart!

Passions are running high when *New York Times* bestselling author Nora Roberts pits a charming ladies' man against his match—this MacKade brother just doesn't know what hit him in *The Fall of Shane MacKade*, the fourth book in Nora's series, THE MACKADE BROTHERS. Trisha Alexander's new series of weddings and babies, THREE BRIDES AND A BABY, begins this month with *A Bride for Luke*. And Joan Elliott Pickart's THE BABY BET series continues in April with *The Father of Her Child*. Rounding out the month is Jennifer Mikels with the tender *Expecting: Baby,* and Judith Yates's warm family tale, *A Will and a Wedding*.

A whole season of love and romance has just begun from Special Edition! I hope you enjoy each and every story to come!

Sincerely,

Tara Gavin
Senior Editor

Please address questions and book requests to:
Silhouette Reader Service
U.S.: 3010 Walden Ave., P.O. Box 1325, Buffalo, NY 14269
Canadian: P.O. Box 609, Fort Erie, Ont. L2A 5X3

Nora Roberts

THE FALL OF SHANE MACKADE

Silhouette®

SPECIAL EDITION®

Published by Silhouette Books

America's Publisher of Contemporary Romance

For those who've taken the fall

 SILHOUETTE BOOKS

ISBN 0-373-24022-8

THE FALL OF SHANE MACKADE

NORA ROBERTS

is one of Silhouette Books' most popular and prolific authors as well as a *New York Times* bestseller. Demand for her early titles was so great they were brought back as part of a special "Language of Love" collection.

Nora was the first author inducted into the Romance Writers of America's Hall of Fame and has received awards for her fiction, her creativity, her sales and her contribution to the genre. She has received lifetime achievement awards from the Romance Writers of America, Waldenbooks and *Romantic Times* magazine, and bestselling title and series awards from booksellers, readers and peers.

Nora Roberts is a consummate storyteller. Her generous spirit, humor, creativity, willingness to take chances and commitment to her characters, her writing and, most especially, her readers, have earned her fame worldwide.

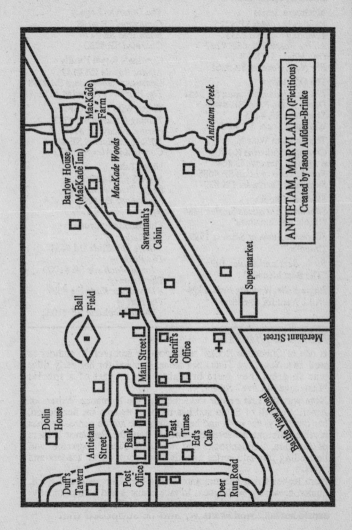

ANTIETAM, MARYLAND (Fictitious)
Created by Jason Aufdem-Brinke

Prologue

Ice covered the shoveled walk from the house to the milking barn, and the path was slick with it. The predawn air was cupped by a dark sky chiseled with frosted chips of white stars. Each gulp was like sipping chilled razor blades that sliced, then numbed, the throat before being expelled in a frigid steam.

Wrapped in a multitude of winter layers, from long johns to knitted muffler, Shane MacKade headed toward the milking parlor and the first chores of the day. Unlike his three older brothers, he was whistling between his teeth.

He just plain loved the frosty and still hour before a winter sunrise.

His oldest brother, Jared, was nearly seventeen, and went about the business of running a farm like an accountant approaching a spreadsheet. It was all figures to him, Shane knew, and he supposed that was well enough. They had lost their father two months before, and times were rough.

As for Rafe, his restless fifteen-year-old soul was already looking beyond the hills and fields of the MacKade farm. The milking and feeding and tending of stock was simply something to get through. And Shane knew, though they never really talked about it, that their father's death had hit Rafe the hardest.

They had all loved their father. It would have been impossible not to love Buck MacKade, with his big voice and big hands and big heart. And everything Shane knew about farming—everything he loved about the land—had come straight from his father.

Perhaps that was why Shane didn't grieve as deeply. The land was there, so his father was there. Always.

He could have talked about that thought with Devin. At fourteen, Devin was already the best of listeners, and the closest to Shane's own age. Shane was going to make the big leap to thirteen next Tuesday. But he kept the thought—and the feeling—to himself.

Inside the milking parlor, the first of the stock shifted and mooed, tails swishing as they were prepped. It was a simple enough process, could even be considered a monotonous one. The cleaning, the feeding, the attaching to machines that would pump the milk from cow to pipe, from pipe to tank for storage. But Shane enjoyed it, enjoyed the smells, the sounds, the routine. While he and Devin dealt with the second line of stock, Rafe and Jared led those already relieved of milk outside again.

They made a good team, quick and efficient despite the numbing cold and early hour. In truth, it was a job any one of them could have handled alone, or with very little help. But they tended to stick together. Even closer together these days.

Still, there were chickens and pigs to see to yet, eggs to gather, muck to shovel, fresh hay to spread. And all this before they gobbled down breakfast and climbed into Jared's ancient car for the drive to school.

If he could have, Shane would have skipped the school part entirely. You couldn't learn how to plow and plant, how to harvest or judge the weather by tasting the air, from books. You couldn't learn from books how to look into a cow's eyes and see that she was ailing.

But his mother was firm on book learning, and when she was firm, she was immovable.

"What the hell are you so happy about?" Grumbling, Rafe clanged stainless-steel buckets together. "That whistling's driving me crazy."

Shane merely grinned and kept on whistling. He paused only long enough to talk encouragingly to the cows. "That's the way, ladies, you fill her up." Content as any of his bossies, Shane moved down the line of milkers, checking each one.

"I'm going to pound him," Rafe announced to no one in particular.

"Leave him be," Devin said mildly. "He's already brain-dead."

Rafe smiled at that. "It's so damn cold, if I hit him, my fingers would probably break off."

"Going to warm up some today." Shane patted one of the cows waiting in the stanchions to be hooked for milking. "Get up into the thirties, anyway."

Rafe didn't bother to ask how Shane knew. Shane always knew. "Big deal." He strode out of the milking parlor, toward barn and hayloft.

"What's eating him?" Shane muttered. "Some girl dump him?"

"He just hates cows." Jared stepped back in, smelling of grain.

"That's stupid. You're a sweetheart, aren't you, baby?" Shane gave the nearest cow an affection swat.

"Shane's in love with cows." Devin flashed the wicked MacKade grin, which had a dimple flickering at the corner of his mouth. "He has better luck kissing them than girls."

Immediately insulted, Shane narrowed his eyes. "I could kiss any girl I wanted to—if I wanted to." Under the layers of clothing, his lean, rangy body was on full alert.

Recognizing the signs, Jared shook his head. He just didn't feel like a tussle now. There was too much work to do, and he had a big test in English Lit to worry about. Devin and Shane were too evenly matched, and a fight between them could go on indefinitely.

"Yeah, you're a regular Don Juan." He said it only to focus Shane's attention, and temper, on him. "All the little girls are puckered up and waiting in line."

Devin made a long, loud kissing noise that made Jared want to slug him. As Shane pivoted to do just that, Jared stepped between them. "But before you make their hearts flutter, lover boy, the water trough's iced over. These cows are thirsty."

Aiming a glance that promised Devin retribution, Shane stomped outside.

He could kiss a girl, Shane thought as he hacked at the ice. If he wanted to. He just wasn't interested.

Well, maybe he was a little interested, he admitted, blowing on his fingers to warm them. Some of the girls he knew were starting to get pretty interesting shapes. And he'd felt an odd sort of tingling under his skin when Jared's girl, Sharilyn, wiggled up against him when they were packed into the front seat of Jared's car the other day.

He could probably kiss her, if he wanted. He set the iron bar aside, looking toward the milk barn as the stars winked out overhead. That would show Jared a thing or two. They all figured he didn't know what was what because he was the youngest. But he knew plenty. At least he was starting to imagine plenty.

Hauling up the bar again, he clumped over the slippery, snowpacked ground to the pig shed.

He knew how sex worked, all right. He'd grown up on a farm, hadn't he? He knew how the bull went crazy and white-eyed when he smelled a cow in heat. He just hadn't thought the whole thing looked like a whole hell of a lot of fun . . . but that had been before he began to notice how girls filled out their clothes.

He hacked away the layer of ice for the pigs and, leaving his brothers to finish up the milking, dealt with the feed.

He wished he was grown-up. He wished he could do something to prove he was—besides holding his own in a fight. As it was, all he could do was simply wait until he was older, and know that then he could take control of his life.

The land was his. He'd felt that in his bones, as long as he could remember. As if at birth someone had whispered it in his ear. The farm, the land. That was what really mattered. And if he wanted a girl, too—or a whole platoon of them—he'd get that, too.

But the farm was what counted most.

The land, he thought, looking over the snow-coated fields as the sky grayed with dawn and turned explosive at the tips of the eastern mountains. The land his father had worked, and his father before that. And before that. Through droughts and floods. Through war.

They'd planted their crops, and brought them in, he thought, dreaming a little as he walked toward the fields. Even when war came, right here, with Confederate gray and Union blue clashing in these very fields, and in the thick woods just beyond, the farm had stayed whole.

He knew just what it would have been like, turning the rocky soil behind a horse-drawn plow, your back and shoulders aching, your hands raw. But the crops would be planted, and you would see them grow. Corn springing up, spreading, hay waving and going gold with summer.

Even when the soldiers came, even when their mortars and black powder singed the drying cornstalks, the land stayed. Bodies had dropped here, he thought as a chill crept up his spine. Men had screamed and crawled through their own blood.

But the land they had fought over, fought for, didn't change. It endured.

He flushed a little, wondering where that word had come from, that word and the strong, almost dizzying emotion behind it. He was glad he was alone, glad none of his brothers could see. He didn't know how to tell them that he knew the farm had been his responsibility before, and would be again.

But he knew.

When he heard the sound behind him, he stiffened and, shouldering the bar again, turned with his face carefully closed, free of emotion.

There was no one there.

He swallowed hard. He was sure he'd heard a sound, a movement, then a small, weak cry. It wasn't the first time he'd heard the ghosts. They lived here, as he did—in the fields, in the woods, in the hills. But they terrified him nonetheless.

Gathering all his young courage, he moved around the shed, toward the old stone smokehouse. It was probably Devin, he told himself, or Rafe, or even Jared, trying to get a rise out of him, trying to make him bolt, as he'd nearly bolted the time they spent the night in the old Barlow place, on the other side of the woods. The haunted house, where ghosts were as thick as cobwebs.

"Get a life, Dev," he said, loudly, loudly enough to calm his speeding heart.

But when he rounded the building, he didn't see his brother, or even any tracks in the snow. For an instant, just a quick, tripping heartbeat, he thought he saw a figure there. Crumpled, spilling blood over the ground, the face as white as the untouched snow, the eyes dulled with pain.

Help me. Please help me, I'm dying.

But when he stepped forward there was nothing. Nothing at all. Even the words that rang in his head faded away in the wind.

Shane stood there, a young boy with his whole life a wonderful mystery yet to unfold, and stared at the unbroken ground. He stood there, shuddering, as the cold reached through the layers of clothes, through his flesh and into his bones.

Then he heard his brothers laughing, heard his mother call from the kitchen door that breakfast was ready and to get a move on or they'd be late for school.

He turned away, closed his frightened mind off to what he had seen and what he had heard.

He walked back to the farmhouse, and said nothing of that one jolting moment to anyone.

Chapter One

Shane MacKade loved women. He loved the look of them, the smell of them, the sound of them, the taste of them. He loved them, without reservation or prejudice. Tall, short, plump, thin, old, young, their wonderful and exotic femaleness pulled him, drew him in. The slant of an eyelash, the curve of a lip, the sway of a shapely female bottom, simply delighted him.

He had, in his thirty-two years on earth, done his very best to show as many women as possible his boundless appreciation for them as a gender.

He considered himself a lucky man, because the ladies loved him right back.

He had other loves. His family, his farm, the smell of bread baking, the taste of a cold beer on a hot day.

But women, well, they were so varied, so different, and so delicious.

He was smiling at one now. Even though Regan was his brother's wife, and Shane had nothing but the most innocent and brotherly feelings for her, he could appreciate her considerable female attributes. He liked the way her deep blond hair curved around her face. He adored the little mole beside her mouth, and the way she always looked so sexy and so tidy at the same time.

He thought if a man had to pick one woman and tie himself down, Rafe couldn't have done better.

"Are you sure you don't mind, Shane?"

"Mind what?" He caught her quirked brow as she lifted the newest MacKade onto her shoulder. "Oh, the airport run. Right. I was just thinking how pretty you look."

Regan had to laugh. She was frazzled, Jason MacKade, her youngest son, was squalling, her hair was a mess, and she was afraid she smelled more like Jason's diapers than the scent she'd dabbed on that morning.

"I look like a madwoman."

"Nope." To give her a breather, Shane took Jason from her and jiggled the three-week-old baby into hiccups. "Just as pretty as ever."

She glanced over to the playpen she'd set up in the back room of her antique shop, where her toddler, Nate, napped through the chaos. He had the look of his father, she thought, with a burst of love. Which meant, of course, that he had the look of his uncle Shane.

"I appreciate it. I can use the flattery. I really hate to ask you, though."

Shane watched her pour tea and resigned himself to drinking it. "It's not a problem, honey. I'll pick up your college pal and get her back to you safe and sound. A scientist, huh?"

"Hmm..." Regan handed him a cup, knowing he could juggle that and his infant nephew and a few more things besides. "Rebecca's brilliant. Over-the-top brilliant. I only roomed with her one year. She was fifteen, and already a sophomore. She ended up graduating, summa cum laude, a full year ahead of me and the rest of her class. Pretty intimidating."

Regan sampled the tea, and the relative quiet now that Shane had Jason calmed down to bubbling coos. "It seemed she was always in some lab, or the library."

"Sounds like a barrel of laughs."

"She was—is—a serious type, and tended to be shy. After all, she was years younger than anyone else in school. But we got to be friends. She'd have come for the wedding, but she was in Europe, or Africa." Regan waved vaguely. "Somewhere."

Shane was thinking nostalgically of his own fifteenth year, when he had learned the intricacies of the back-hook bra. In the dark. "It's nice you've got a pal coming to visit."

"Well, it's kind of a working visit for her." Regan gnawed her lip. She hadn't mentioned Rebecca's purpose, except to Rafe. She supposed if she was going to dragoon Shane into meeting her friend at the airport, she ought to make it clear.

She studied him as he made faces at the baby, then nuzzled Jason. All the MacKades were stunners, she thought, but there was something about Shane. Just an extra slice of charm, she supposed.

He had the looks, of course. That thick, midnight-black hair that he now wore in a stubby ponytail. The

thin, bony, mouth-watering face, with its angles and
planes, lush mouth, flashing dimple and thickly
lashed green eyes. His shade of green was dreamy, the
shade of an ocean at twilight.

He had the build—tall, rangy, muscled. Broad
shoulders, narrow hips, long, long legs. It showed to
advantage in jeans and work boots and flannel.

He had the charm. All four MacKades had it to
spare, but Regan thought there was an extra dollop in
Shane. Something about the way his eyes lingered on
a woman, the quick, appreciative grin when he spoke
to one, be she eight or eighty. That easygoing, cheerful manner that could explode into temper, then, just
as quickly, edge away into a laugh.

He'd probably scare the hell out of poor, shy Rebecca.

"You're awfully good with him," she murmured.

"You keep making babies, honey, I'll keep loving
them."

Amused, she angled her head. "Still not ready to
settle down?"

"Now why would I want to go and do that?" He
looked up from Jason, and his eyes danced with humor. "I'm the last single MacKade. I'm honor-bound
to hold the fort until the nephews start springing up."

"And you take your duty seriously."

"You bet. He's asleep." Shane lowered his head
and kissed Jason's brow. "Want me to put him
down?"

"Thanks." She waited until Shane had Jason settled in the antique cradle. "Rebecca's expecting me.
I wasn't able to catch her before she left for the airport." Frazzled all over again, Regan ran her fingers
though her hair. "The baby-sitter canceled, Rafe's in

Hagerstown getting building material. Cassie's got a full house over at the inn, Emma's got the sniffles, and I just couldn't ask Savannah to help out."

"Last time I saw her, she looked ready to pop." To demonstrate the condition of Jared's wife, Shane made a wide circle with his arms in front of his flat belly.

"Exactly. She's too pregnant to drive a three-hour round trip, and with a furniture delivery being re-scheduled for this afternoon, I didn't know who else to call and impose on."

"It's no trouble." To prove it, he kissed the tip of her nose. "I don't suppose she's as pretty as you, is she?"

Regan chuckled at that. "How am I supposed to answer that and not sound like a jerk? In any case, I haven't seen her in...five years, I guess. The last time was on a quick trip to New York, and she was hip-deep in some paper she was writing. She's four years younger than I am and has two doctorates. Maybe more. I can't keep up."

Shane didn't wince. He liked women with brains as much as he liked women without them. But he knew the old routine about smarts and wonderful person-alities. He didn't think he was going to be picking up a beauty queen at the airport.

"Psychiatry and U.S. history for sure," Regan continued. "Kind of an odd mix, but then, Rebec-ca's unique. I remember she minored in some sort of complex math, and there was science, too. Physics, chemistry... she did postgrad work on that at MIT."

"Why?" Shane wondered out loud.

"With Rebecca it would be more a matter of why not. She's got what they call a photographic memory. Sees it, reads it, files it up there," Regan said, tapping her head.

"And she's a shrink?"

"She doesn't have a private practice. She consults, writes papers, lectures. I know she used to donate a day a week to a clinic. She wrote a definitive paper on . . . well, some psychosis or other. Or maybe it was a phobia. I'm a business major. Anyway, Shane—" Regan smiled brightly and patted his hand "—she's into parapsychology. As a hobby."

"Into what? Is that like ghostbusting?"

"It's the study of the paranormal. ESP, psychic phenomena, ah . . . hauntings . . ."

"Ghosts," Shane concluded, and this time he did wince. "Don't we have enough of that around here already?"

"That's the point. She's interested in the area, the legends. It's different for you, Shane," Regan hurried on, knowing her brother-in-law's aversion to local legends. "You grew up with it all. The Barlow House, the two corporals, the haunted woods. The whole idea of hauntings is one of the main reasons Rafe and I have been able to make such a success out of the inn. People love the idea of staying in a haunted house."

Shane only shrugged. Hell, he *lived* in one. "I don't mind all that. It's just when tourists want to go tramping around the farm that—"

The look in her eye stopped him, made him narrow his own. "She wants to tramp around the farm."

"She wants the whole picture, and I know she'd like to spend some time out there. But that's totally up to you," Regan said quickly. "You need to get to know her a little. She's really a fascinating woman.

Anyway, I wrote down her flight number and so forth." Regan offered him a sheet of paper.

"You still haven't told me what she looks like. I doubt she's going to be the only woman off that flight from New York."

"Right. Brown hair, brown eyes. She used to wear it just sort of pulled back, or... hanging down. She's about my height, thin—"

"Skinny or slim? There's a difference."

"I guess more on the skinny side. She may be wearing glasses. She uses them to read, but she used to forget to take them off and she'd end up running into things."

"A skinny, clumsy brunette with glasses. Got it."

"She's very attractive," Regan added loyally. "In a unique way. And, Shane? She's shy, so be nice."

"I'm always nice. To women."

"All right, be good then. If you don't spot her, you can have her paged. Dr. Rebecca Knight."

Airports always entertained Shane. People were in just as much of a hurry, it seemed to him, to get where they were going as they were to get back from wherever they'd been. Everyone hit the ground running, loaded down with carryons. He wondered what it was about the places people chose to leave that didn't appeal enough to keep them there.

Not that he was against travel. He just figured he could get anywhere he really wanted to go by sitting behind the wheel of his pickup. That way, he was in charge of time and distance and speed.

But it took all kinds.

He also figured he could spot Regan's college pal—since she was a woman, and he knew women. She'd be in her mid-twenties, about five foot five, skinny, brown hair, brown eyes, probably behind thick glasses. From Regan's brief rundown, he didn't imagine Rebecca Knight had a great deal of style, so he would look for a plain, intellectual type, with a briefcase and practical shoes.

He loitered at the gate, eyeing a pair of flight attendants who were waiting for a change of crew. Now that, he mused, was a profession that drew pretty women. It almost made a man feel there'd be some advantage in being stuck in a flying tin can for a few hours.

As passengers began to pour out of the gateway, he judiciously shifted his attention. Businessmen, looking harried, he noted. The suit-and-tie brigade. No amount of money could convince him that it would be worth wearing a suit for eight to ten hours a day. Nice-looking blonde in sleek red slacks. She gave him a quick, flirtatious smile as she passed, and Shane pleased himself by drawing in the cloud of scent she left behind.

Pretty brunette with a long, ground-eating stride and big, wide gold eyes. They reminded him of the amber beads his mother had kept in her good jewelry box.

Here came Grandma, with an enormous shopping bag and a huge, misty-eyed grin for the trio of children who raced up to hug her knees.

Ah, there she is, Shane decided, spotting a slump-shouldered woman with brown hair scraped back in a frowsy knot. She carried an official-looking black briefcase and wore thick, laced shoes and square glasses. She blinked owlishly behind them, looking lost.

"Hey." He gave her a quick, flashing smile, and a friendly wink that had her backing up three steps into a frazzled man lugging a bulging garment bag. "How's it going?" He reached down to take her briefcase and had her myopic eyes going round with alarm. "I'm Shane. Regan sent me to fetch you. She had complications. So how was the flight?"

"I—I—" The woman pulled her briefcase protectively against her thin chest. "I'll call Security."

"Take it easy, Becky. I'm just going to give you a ride."

She opened her mouth and made a squeaking noise. When Shane reached out for her arm to reassure her, she gave him a solid thwack with the briefcase. Before he had decided whether to laugh or swear, he felt a light tap on his arm.

"Excuse me." The pretty brunette cocked a brow and gave him a long, considering study. "I believe you may be looking for me." Her mouth, which Shane noted was wide and full, curved into a dryly amused smile. "Shane, you said. That would be Shane MacKade?"

"Yeah. Oh." He glanced back at the woman he'd accosted. "Sorry," he began, but she was already darting off like a rabbit pursued by wolves.

"I imagine that's the most excitement she's had in some time," Rebecca commented. She thought she knew just how the poor woman had felt. It was so miserable to be shy and plain and not quite in step with the rest of the world. "I'm Rebecca Knight," she added, and thrust out a hand.

She wasn't quite what he'd expected, but on closer study he saw he hadn't been that far off. She did look intellectual, if you got past those eyes. Rather than practical shoes, it was a practical haircut, as short as a boy's. He preferred hair on a woman, personally, but this chopped-off 'do suited her face, with its pointy, almost foxlike features.

And she was probably skinny. It was just hard to tell, with the boxy, shape-disguising jacket and slacks, all in unrelieved black.

So he smiled again, taking the long, narrow hand in his. "Regan said your eyes were brown. They're not."

"It says they are on my driver's license. Is Regan all right?"

"She's fine. Just some domestic and professional complications. Here, let me take that." He reached for the big, many-pocketed bag she had slung over her shoulder.

"No thanks, I've got it. You're one of the brothers-in-law."

"Yeah." He took her arm to steer her around toward the terminal.

Strong fingers, she noted. And a predilection for touching. Well, that was all right. She wouldn't squeak, as the other woman had—as she herself might have a few months before, when faced with a pure, unadulterated male.

"The one who runs the farm."

"That's right. You don't look much like a Ph.D.— on first glance."

"Don't I?" She sent him a cool sidelong look. She'd done a lot of mirror-practicing on that look. "And the woman who is probably even now hyperventilating in the nearest ladies' room did?"

"It was the shoes," Shane explained, and grinned down at Rebecca's neat black canvas flats.

"I see." As they rode down the escalator toward Baggage Claim, she turned to face him. Flannel shirt open at the collar, she noted. Worn jeans, scarred boots, big, callused hands. Thick black hair spilling out of a battered cap, on top of a lean, tanned face that could have been on a poster selling anything.

"You look like a farmer," she decided. "So how long a drive is it to Antietam?"

He debated whether or not he'd been insulted or complimented and answered, "Just over an hour. We'll get your bags."

"They're being sent." Pleased with her practicality, she patted the bag over her arm. "This is all I have at the moment."

Shane couldn't get over the sensation—the uncomfortable sensation—that he was being observed, sized up and dissected like a laboratory frog. "Great." It relieved him when she took shaded glasses from her jacket pocket and slipped them on.

He was used to women looking at him, but not as though he were something smeared on a slide.

When they reached his truck, she gave it a brief look, then gave him another as he opened the door for her. She granted him one of those cool smiles, then tipped down her glasses to peer at him over them.

"Oh, one thing, Shane..."

Because she'd paused, he frowned a little. "Yeah?"

"Nobody calls me Becky."

With that she slid neatly onto the seat and set her bag on the floor.

She enjoyed the ride. He drove well, and the truck ran smoothly. And she couldn't help but get a little glow of satisfaction at having annoyed him, just a bit. Men who not only looked as good as Shane Mac-Kade but had the extra bonus of exuding all that sex and confidence weren't easy to take down a peg.

She'd spent a lot of her life being intimidated on any kind of social level. Only in the past few months had she begun to make progress toward holding her own. She'd become her own project, and Rebecca thought she was coming along very well.

She gave him credit for making easy conversation on the trip, annoyed or not. Before long they were off the highway and driving on winding back roads. It was a pretty picture, hills and houses, pastures and trees that held their lush summer green into the late, hazy August, an occasional horse or grazing cow.

He'd turned the radio music politely low, and all she could really hear from the speakers was the throb of the beat.

The cab of the truck was neat, with the occasional strand of golden dog hair drifting upward, and the scent of dog with it. There were a couple of scribbled notes attached by magnet to the metal dash, a handful of coins tossed into the ashtray. But it was ordered.

Perhaps that was why she spotted the little gold twist of a woman's earring peeking out from under the floor mat. She reached down and plucked it up.

"Yours?"

He flicked a glance, caught the glint of gold and remembered that Frannie Spader had been wearing earrings like that the last time they... took a drive together.

"A friend's." Shane held out his hand. When the earring was in it, he dropped it carelessly amid the coins.

"She'll want it back," Rebecca noted idly. "It's fourteen-karat. So... there are four of you, right?"

"Yep. Do you have any brothers, sisters?"

"No. But you run the family farm?"

"That's the way it worked out. Jared has his law practice, Rafe's into building, Devin's the sheriff."

"And you're the farm boy," she finished. "What do you farm?"

"We have dairy cattle, pigs. Grow corn—feed mostly, but some nice Silver Queen—hay, alfalfa." He could see she was taking it all in with those big intense eyes, and he added, very soberly, "We've had ourselves a nice crop of potatoes."

"Really?" In unconscious sympathy with the beat whispering through the speakers, she drummed her fingers on her knee. "Isn't that a lot of work for one man?"

"My brothers are there when they're needed. And I take on some 4-H students seasonally." He moved his shoulders. "I've got a couple of nephews coming up. They're eleven now. I can usually con them into believing they're having fun when they're feeding the stock."

"And is it fun?"

"I like it." This time he looked at her. "Ever been on a farm?"

"No, not really. I'm an urbanite."

"Then you're in for a surprise with Antietam," he murmured. "Urban it's not."

"So Regan tells me. And, of course, I know the area through my studies. It must have been interesting growing up on one of the major battlefields of the Civil War.''

"Rafe was always more into that than me. The land doesn't care if it's historical, as long as it's tended.''

"So you're not interested in the history?''

"Not particularly." The truck rumbled over the bridge that spanned the piece of the Potomac River between Virginia and Maryland. "I know it," he added. "You can't live there all your life and not know it. But I don't give it a lot of attention.''

"And the ghosts?''

"I don't give them a lot of attention, either.''

A smile shadowed her mouth. "But you know of them.''

Again he moved his shoulders. "Part of the package. You want to talk to the rest of the family about that. They're more into it.''

"Yet you live and work on a farm that's supposedly haunted.''

"Supposedly." He didn't care to talk about it, or think about it. "Look, Regan mentioned something about you coming out to do whatever it is you do—''

"To study and record any paranormal activity." Her smile spread. "It's just a hobby.''

"Yeah, well, you'd be better off at the old Barlow place, the house Rafe and Regan put back together. It's a bed-and-breakfast now—one of my other sisters-in-law runs it. It's lousy with ghosts, if you believe in that sort of thing.''

"Mmm . . . It's on my list. In fact, I'm hoping they can squeeze me in for a while. I'd like to stay there. And from what Regan told me, you have a large house. I'd like to stay there, too.''

He wouldn't mind the company, but the purpose didn't sit well with him. "Regan didn't mention how long you were planning on being around."

"That depends." She looked out the window as he took a route through a cut in the mountains. "It depends on how long it takes me to find what I want to find, and how long it takes to document it."

"Don't you have, like, a job?"

"I'm taking a sabbatical." The word had such marvelous possibilities, she closed her eyes to savor them. "I have all the time in the world, and I intend to enjoy it." Opening her eyes again, she saw the glint from the little gold earring in the ashtray. "Don't worry, farm boy. I won't cramp your style. When the time comes, you can tuck me into some little room in the attic. I'll do my thing, you can do yours."

He started to comment, but she made some soft, strangled sound and sat bolt upright in the seat. "What?"

She could only shake her head, absorbed in the jarring sense of déjà vu. The hills rose up, grass green against outcroppings of silver rocks. In the distance, the higher mountains were purple shadows against hazy skies. Fields, high with green stalks of corn, thick with summer grains, rolled back from the road. On a sloping embankment, black-and-white cows stood as still as if they were on a postcard.

Woods, dark and thick, ranged along a field, while a winding creek bubbled along the verge.

"It looks just as it should," she murmured softly. "Exactly. Perfect."

"Thanks. It's MacKade land." He slowed the truck a little, out of pride. "You can't see the house this time of year. Trees are too thick. It's back down that lane.''

She saw the rough gravel road, the way it swung left and followed the line of trees. With her heart thudding dully in her breast, she nodded.

Come hell or high water, she thought, she was going back there. And she would stay until she found all the answers to all the questions that plagued her.

She took a deep breath, turned to him. ''How far to town?''

''Just a few miles now.'' His eyes narrowed with concern. She'd gone dead pale. ''You all right?''

''I'm fine.'' But she did open the window to take a deep gulp of late summer. ''I'm just fine.''

Chapter Two

Through the display window of her shop, Regan saw the truck pull up to the curb. With a child in each arm, she dashed outside.

"Dr. Knight."

"Mrs. MacKade." Rebecca slid out of the cab of the truck and let out a cry of pure pleasure, then launched herself at her friend as her vision blurred.

Gone was the cool and the clinical, Shane noted, and he found himself grinning at the way the two women babbled and embraced. He'd had some reservations about Rebecca Knight—and maybe he'd keep a few of them. But there was no doubt as to the depth of affection here.

"Oh, I've missed you. I've missed you," Rebecca said over and over as tears stung her eyes. "Oh, Regan, you're so gorgeous, and look at these. Your babies."

She let the tears come. She'd never had to hold back or feel foolish with Regan. Sniffling, she touched Nate's cheek, then stroked a finger along the baby's soft head.

"I don't see you for a few years, and look what you do. Married and the mother of two. I've got to hold one."

Always willing, Nate held out his arms.

"You must look like your daddy," Rebecca commented, delighted when Nate puckered up for a kiss.

"Daddy," Nate agreed. "Play ball. Shane!" He bounced up and down like a spring. "Shane, gimme ride."

"Shows what you know, choosing your uncle over a lady." But Shane hauled Nate onto his shoulders, where the toddler could squeal and grip his hair.

"You found each other." Regan beamed at both of them. "I'm sorry I couldn't get away to pick you up myself."

"I'd say you had your hands full." Rebecca turned to give Shane a mild smile. "And your brother-in-law managed just fine. All in all."

"You must be tired. Come into the shop. I'm just closing up. Shane, come in for some tea."

"I have to get back, thanks anyway. Down you go, Nate." He swung the boy around, inciting a series of rolling belly laughs.

Wise to her son, Regan clutched Nate's hand firmly in hers the minute his little feet hit the ground. "Thanks." She kissed Shane lightly on the lips. "I owe you one. I want to give Rebecca a welcome dinner tomorrow, when she's had time to catch her breath. You'll come, won't you?"

"A free meal." He winked. "Count on it. See you."

"Thanks for the lift. Farm boy."

Shane paused at the driver's-side door. "Anytime. Becky."

Regan lifted a brow as he drove away. "Becky?"

"Just a little joke." Objectively she looked up and down the street, noted the light traffic, the old stone buildings, the people loitering in front of doorways. "I'm trying to picture Regan Bishop as resident and shop owner of Small Town, U.S.A."

"It was home the minute I saw it. Come inside," she said again. "Tell me what you think of the shop."

Now she could picture it, Rebecca realized the moment she stepped into Past Times. The style, the elegance of gleaming antiques, lovely old lamps and glass and statuary. There was a smell of spice and baby powder that made her smile.

"Mama," she said after turning around in a circle. "How does it feel?"

"Incredible. I can't wait for you to meet Rafe." She moved into a back room, setting the baby in a bassinet, then lifting Nate into a high chair, where he occupied himself with a cookie. It gave her time to take a breath. "Of course, you've seen Shane, so you've got a fairly good idea of the MacKade looks."

"Are they all like that?"

"Tall, dark and ridiculously handsome? Every one of them. With bad-boy reputations to match." She leaned back, took a long survey. "Rebecca, it's always what people say when they haven't seen in other for a while, but I have to say it anyway. You look wonderful."

Rebecca smiled as she tugged on a short tress of chestnut-brown hair. "I got the nerve to have this hacked off when I was in Europe a few months ago. You were always trying to coax me into doing something with my hair."

"I'd have never been that brave, or inventive. Boy, it suits you, Rebecca. And—"

"The clothes?" Her smile widened. "That was Europe, too. I had a crisis of style, so to speak. I was walking along the Left Bank and happened to catch a glimpse of this woman reflected in one of the shop windows. She looked like an unkempt scarecrow. Her hair was tangled and hanging down in her face, and she had on the most dreadful brown suit. I thought, *Poor thing, to look like that in a city like this*. And then I realized it was me."

"You're too hard on yourself."

"I was a mess," Rebecca said firmly. "A cliché, the dowdy prodigy with a sharp brain and bad shoes. I walked into the nearest beauty salon, gave myself no time to think, to rationalize, to intellectualize, and threw myself on their mercy. Who'd have thought a decent haircut could make such a difference to the way I felt? It seemed so shallow. I told myself that even when I walked out with several hundred dollars' worth of skin creams."

She laughed at herself as she realized that, after all this time, she was still savoring that moment. "Then I realized that if appearances weren't important, it couldn't be a problem to present a good one."

"Then I'll say it again. You look wonderful." Regan reached out for Rebecca's hands. "In fact, since you're happy with the change, I'll be perfectly honest and tell you I wouldn't have recognized you.

You're absolutely striking, and I'm so glad to see you looking so fabulous.''

"I have to say this." She gave Regan's hands a hard squeeze. "Regan, you were my first real friend.''

"Rebecca.''

"My very first, the only person I was close to who didn't treat me like an oddity. I've wanted to tell you for a long time what that meant to me. What you meant to me. But even with you, I had a hard time getting that kind of thing out.''

"You're making me cry again," Regan managed.

"There's more. I was so nervous coming here, worrying that the friendship, the connection, might not be the same. But it is. Hell." Rebecca gave a lavish sniff. "Got any tissue?''

Regan dived into a diaper bag and pulled out a travel pack. She handed a tissue to Rebecca, used one herself. "I'm so happy," she said, weeping.

"Me too.''

Rebecca decided the rambling old stone house just outside of town suited Regan and Rafe MacKade perfectly. It had the rough, masculine charm of Rafe MacKade, and the style and feminine grace of Regan, all rolled into one.

She would have spotted Rafe as Shane's brother from a mile away with one eye closed, so powerful was the resemblance. So she wasn't surprised when he pulled her into his arms for a hard hug the moment he saw her.

She'd already gleaned that the MacKades liked women.

"Regan's been fretting and fussing for two weeks," he told Rebecca over a glass of wine in the big, airy living room.

"I have not been fussing or fretting."

Rafe smiled and, from his seat on the sofa, reached up to stroke his wife's hand as she sat on the arm near him. "She polished everything twice, vacuumed up every dog hair." He gave the golden retriever slumbering on the rug an affection nudge with his foot.

"*Most* of the dog hair," Regan corrected.

"I'm flattered." Rebecca jolted a little when Nate knocked over his building blocks and sent them scattering.

"Attaboy," Rafe said mildly. "If it's not built right, just tear it down and start again."

"Daddy. Come play."

"It's all in the foundation," Rafe said as he got up and ranged himself on the floor with his son. They began to move blocks, Rafe's big hands moving with Nate's small, pudgy ones. "Regan says you want a close-up look at the inn."

"I do. I want to stay there, at least for a while, if you have a vacancy."

"Oh, but . . . we want you here, Rebecca."

Rebecca smiled over at Regan. "I appreciate that, and I do want to spent time here, as well. But it would really help if I could stay a few nights there, anyway."

"Ghostbusting," Rafe said, with a wink at his son.

"If you like," Rebecca returned coolly.

"Hey, don't get me wrong. They're there. The first time I got a good hold of Regan was when I caught her as she was fainting in the hallway of the inn. They'd spooked her."

"That's not entirely true," Regan said. "I thought Rafe was playing a prank, and when I realized he wasn't, I got...overwrought."

"Tell me about it." Fascinated, Rebecca leaned forward. "What did you see?"

"I didn't see anything." Regan blew out a breath. Her son was too involved with his blocks to notice the subject of the conversation. And, in any case, he was a MacKade. "It was more a feeling...of not being alone. The house had been deserted and empty for years then. Rafe hadn't even begun the renovations. But there were noises. Footsteps, a door closing. There's a spot on the stairs, a cold spot."

"You felt it?" Rebecca's voice was flat now, that of a scientist assessing data.

"Right to the bone. It was so shocking. Rafe told me later that a young Confederate soldier had been killed there, on the day of the Battle of Antietam."

"The two corporals." Rebecca nodded at Regan's surprised look. "I've been researching the area, the legends. Two soldiers, from opposite sides, met in the woods on September 17, 1862. It's thought they were lost, or perhaps deserting. They were both very young. They fought there, wounded each other badly. One made his way to the home of Charles Barlow, now the MacKade Inn. The mistress of the house, Abigail, was a Southern woman, wed to a Yankee businessman. She had the wounded boy brought inside, and was having him carried upstairs to be tended. Instead, her husband came down and shot and killed him, there on the stairs."

"That's right," Regan agreed. "You'll often smell roses in the house. Abigail's roses."

"Really." Rebecca mulled the information over. "Well, well . . . Isn't that fascinating." Her eyes went dreamy for a moment, then sharpened again. "I managed to contact a descendant of one of the Barlow servants who was there at the time. It seems Abigail did her best to take care of the boy, even after his death. She had the servants search his pockets and they found some letters. She wrote to his parents and arranged for his body to be taken back home for burial."

"I never knew that," Regan murmured.

"Abigail kept it as quiet as possible, likely to avoid her husband's wrath. The boy's name was Gray, Franklin Gray, Corporal, CSA, and he never saw his nineteenth birthday."

"Some people hear the shot, and weeping. Cassie—that's Devin's wife—runs the inn for us. She can tell you more."

"I'd like to see the place tomorrow, if I can. And the woods. I need to see the farm, too. The other corporal, name unknown, was buried by the MacKades. I hope to find out more. My equipment should be here by late tomorrow, or the next day."

"Equipment?" Rafe asked.

"Sensors, cameras, temperature gauges. Parapsychology is best approached as a science. Tell me, have there been any reports of telekinetic activities—the movement of inanimate objects? Poltergeists?"

"No." Regan gave a quick shudder. "And I'm sure we'd have heard."

"Well, I can always hope."

Baffled, Regan stared at her. "You used to be so . . ."

"Serious-minded? I still am. Believe me, I'm very serious about this."

"Okay." With a quick shake of her head, Regan rose. "And I better get serious about dinner."

"I'll give you a hand."

Regan arched a brow as Rebecca stood. "Don't tell me you learned to cook in Europe, too."

"No, I can't boil an egg."

"You used to say it was genetic."

"I remember. Now I think it's just a phobia. Cooking's a dangerous business. Sharp edges, heat, flame. But I remember how to set a table."

"Good enough."

Late that night, when Rebecca settled into her room, she snuggled up on the big padded window seat with a book and a cup of Regan's tea. From down the hall she dimly heard the sound of a baby's fretful crying, then footsteps padding down the hall. Within moments the quiet returned as, Rebecca imagined, Regan nursed the baby. She'd never imagined the Regan Bishop she'd known as a mother. In college, Regan had always been bright, energetic, interested in everyone and everything. Of course, she'd attracted male companionship, Rebecca remembered with a small smile. A woman who looked like Regan would always draw men. But it was not merely Regan's beauty, but her way with people, that had made her so popular with both men and women.

And Rebecca, dowdy, serious-minded, out-of-place Rebecca, had been so shocked, and so dazzled, when Regan offered her friendship. She'd been so miserably shy, Rebecca thought now, staring dreamily out the window while the cup warmed her hands. Still was, she admitted, beneath the veneer she'd developed in recent months. She'd had no social skills whatsoever then, and no defense against the fast-moving college scene.

Except for Regan, who had found it natural to take a young, awkward, unattractive girl under her wing.

It was something Rebecca would never forget. And sitting there, in the lovely guest room, with its big four-poster and lovely globe lamps, she was deeply, warmly happy that Regan had found such a wonderful life.

A man who adored her, obviously, Rebecca thought. Anyone could see Rafe's love for his wife every time he looked in her direction.

A strong, handsome, fascinating man, two delightful children, a successful business, a beautiful home. Yes, she was thrilled to find Regan so content.

As for herself, contentment had been eluding her of late. Academia, which had encompassed her all her life, had lately become more of a prison than a home. And, in truth, it was the only home she had ever known. Yet she'd fled from it. For a few months, at least, she felt compelled to explore facets of herself other than her intellect.

She wanted feelings, emotions, passions. She wanted to take risks, make mistakes, do foolish and exciting things.

Perhaps it was the dreams, those odd, recurring dreams, that had influenced her. Whatever it was, the fact that her closest friend had settled in Antietam, a place of history and legend, had been too tempting to resist.

It not only gave her the opportunity to visit, and recement an important relationship, it offered her the chance to delve more deeply into a hobby that was quickly becoming a compulsion.

She couldn't really put her finger on when and how the study of the paranormal had begun to appeal to her. It seemed to have been a gradual thing, an article here, a question there.

Then, of course, the dreams. They had started several years before—odd little snippets of imagery that had seemed like memories. Over time, the dreams had lengthened and increased in clarity.

And she'd begun to document them. After all, as a psychiatrist, she understood the value of dreams. As a scientist, she respected the strength of the unconscious. She'd approached the entire matter as she would any project—in an organized, precise and objective manner. But her objectivity had been systematically overcome by pure curiosity.

So, she was here. Was it coincidence, imagination or fate that made her believe she'd come to a place she was meant to come to? Had been drawn to?

She would see.

Meanwhile, she would enjoy it. The time with Regan, the beauty of the countryside, the professional and personal delight of standing on historic land. She would indulge herself in her hobby, work on her confidence and explore the possibilities.

She thought she'd done well with Shane Mac-Kade. There had been a time, not so terribly long ago, when she would have stammered and flushed, or mumbled and hunched her shoulders in the presence of a man that . . . male. Her tongue would have thickened and tied itself into knots at the terrifying prospect of making conversation that wasn't academic in nature.

But she'd not only talked with him, she'd held her own. And, for the most part, she'd felt comfortable doing so. She'd even joked with him, and she thought she might try her hand at flirting next.

What could it hurt, after all?

Amused at the idea, she got up and climbed under the wedding-ring quilt. She didn't feel like reading, and refused to feel guilty that she wasn't going to end the day with some intellectual stimulus. Instead, she closed her eyes and enjoyed the feel of the smooth sheets against her skin, the soft, cushiony give of down-filled pillows under her cheek, the spicy scent of the bouquet in the vase on the dresser across the room.

She was teaching herself to take time to enjoy textures, scents, sounds. Just now she could hear the wind sigh against the windows, the creak and groan of boards settling, the gentle swish of her leg moving over the sheet.

Small things, she thought with a smile ghosting around her mouth. The small things she had never taken time to appreciate. The new Rebecca Knight took the time and appreciated very much.

Before snuggling deeper, she reached out to switch the lamp off. In the dark, she let her mind wander to what pleasures she might explore the next day. A trip to the inn, certainly. She was looking forward to seeing the haunted house, meeting Cassie MacKade. And Devin, she mused. He was the brother married to the inn's manager. He was also the sheriff, she mused. Probably a good man to know.

With luck, they would have a room for her, and she could set up her equipment as soon as it arrived. But even if not, she was sure she could arrange for a tour of the inn, and add some stories to her file.

She wanted a walk in the woods, again reputedly haunted. She hoped someone could point out the area where the two corporals had supposedly met and fought.

The way Regan had explained the layout, Rebecca thought she might slip through the woods and get a firsthand look at the MacKade farm. She wanted badly to see if she had a reaction to it, the way she had when Shane drove by the land that bordered the road.

So familiar, she thought sleepily. The trees and rocks, the gurgle of the creek. All so oddly familiar.

It could be explained, she supposed. She had visited the battlefield years before. She remembered walking the fields, studying the monuments, reenacting every step of the engagement in her head. She didn't remember passing that particular stretch of road, but she might have, while she was tucked into the back seat of the family car being quizzed by her parents.

No, the woods wouldn't have beckoned to her then. She would have been too busy absorbing data, analyzing it and reporting it to take note of the shape and color of the leaves, the sound of the creek hurrying over rocks.

She would make up for that tomorrow. She would make up for a great many things.

So she drifted into sleep, dreaming of possibilities....

It was terrible, terrible, to hear the sounds of war. It was heart-wrenching to know that so many young men were fighting, dying. Dying as her Johnnie had—her tall, beautiful son, who would never smile at her again, never sneak into the kitchen for an extra biscuit.

As the sounds of battle echoed in the distance, Sarah forced back fear, forced herself to go on with the routine of stirring the stew she had simmering over the fire. And to remind herself that she had had Johnnie for eighteen wonderful years. No one could take her memories of him away. God had also given her two beautiful daughters, and that was a comfort.

She worried about her husband. She knew he ached for their dead son every day, every night. The battle that had come so frighteningly close to home was only one more cruel reminder of what war cost.

He was such a good man, she thought, wiping her hands on her apron. Her John was strong and kind, and her love for him was as full and rich as it had been twenty years before, when she took his ring and his name. And she never doubted his love for her.

After all these years, her heart still leaped when he walked into the room, and her needs still jumped whenever he turned to her in the night. She knew all women weren't as fortunate.

But she worried about him. He didn't laugh as freely since the terrible day they'd gotten word that Johnnie had been lost at Bull Run. There were lines around his eyes, and a bitterness in them that hadn't been there before.

Johnnie had gone for the South—rashly, idealistically—and his father had been so proud of him.

It was true enough that in this border state of Maryland, there were Southern sympathizers, and families ripped in two as they chose sides. But there had been no sides in the MacKade family. Johnnie had made his choice with his father's support. And the choice had killed him.

It was that she feared most. That John blamed himself, as well as the Yankees. That he would never be able to forgive either one, and would never be truly at peace again.

She knew that if it hadn't been for her and the girls, he would have left the farm to fight. It frightened her that there was the need inside him to take up arms, to kill. It was the one thing in their lives they never discussed.

She arched her back, placing the flat of her hand at the base of her spine to ease a dull ache. It reassured her to hear her daughters talking as they peeled potatoes and carrots for the stew. She understood that their incessant chatter was to help block the nerves that jumped at hearing mortar fire echo in the air.

They'd lost half a cornfield this morning—the fighting had come that close. She thanked God it had veered off again and she wasn't huddled in the root cellar with her children. That John was safe. She couldn't bear to lose another she loved.

When John came in, she poured him coffee. There was such weariness in his face, she set the cup aside and went over to wrap her arms around him instead. He smelled of hay and animals and sweat, and his arms were strong as they returned the embrace.

"It's moving off, Sarah." His lips brushed her cheek. "I don't want you fretting."

"I'm not fretting." Then she smiled as he arched one silver-flecked black brow. "Only a little."

He brushed his thumb under her eye, over the shadows that haunted there. "More than a little.

Damn war. Damn Yankees. What gives them the right to come on my land and do their killing? Bastards." He turned away and picked up his coffee.

Sarah sent her daughters a look that had them getting up quietly and leaving the room.

"They're going now," she murmured. "The firing is getting farther and farther away. It can't last much longer."

He knew she wasn't talking about this one battle, and shook his head. The bitterness was back in his eyes. "It'll last as long as they want it to last. As long as men have sons to die. I need to go check things." He set down the coffee without having tasted it. "I don't want you or the girls setting foot out of the house."

"John." She reached for his hand, holding the hard, callused palm against hers. What could she say? That there was no one to blame? Of course there was, but the men who manufactured war and death were nameless and faceless to her. Instead, she brought his hand to her cheek. "I love you."

"Sarah." For a moment, for her, his eyes softened. "Pretty Sarah." His lips brushed hers before he left her.

In sleep, Rebecca stirred, shifted and murmured.

John left the house knowing there was little he could do. In the distance, drying cornstalks were blackened and hacked. He knew there would be blood seeping into his ground. And didn't want to know whether the men who had died there had been taken away yet or not.

It was his land, his, damn them. When he plowed in the spring, he knew, he would be haunted by the blood and death he turned into the earth.

He reached into his pocket, closing his hand over the miniature of his son that he always carried. He didn't weep; his eyes were dry and hard as they scanned the land. Without the land, he was nothing. Without Sarah, he would be lost. Without his daughters, he would willingly die.

But now he had no choice but to live without his boy.

Grim-faced, he stood there, his hands in his pockets, his eyes on his land. When he heard the whimpering, his brows drew together. He'd already checked the stock, secured them. Had he missed a calf? Or had one of his dogs broken out of the stall he'd locked them in to keep them from being hit by a stray bullet?

He followed the sound to the smokehouse, afraid he would have a wounded animal to tend or put down. Though he'd been a farmer all his life, he still was struck with guilt and grief whenever it was necessary to put an animal out of its misery.

But it wasn't an animal, it was a man. A damn bluebelly, bleeding his guts out on MacKade land. For an instant, he felt a hot rush of pleasure. Die here, he thought. Die here, the way my son died on another man's land. You might have been the one to kill him.

Without sympathy, he used his boot to shove the man over onto his back. The Union uniform was filthy, soaked with blood. He was glad to see it, coldly thrilled.

Then he saw the face, and it wasn't a man. It was a boy. His soft cheeks were gray with pain, his eyes glazed with it. Then they fixed on John's.

"Daddy? Daddy, I came home."

"I ain't your daddy, boy."

The eyes closed. "Help me. Please help me. I'm dying...."

In sleep, Shane's fist curled in the sheets, and his restless body tangled them.

Chapter Three

It was one of the most exciting moments of Rebecca's life—just to stand in the balmy air, a vivid blue sky overhead and the old stone house spreading out in front of her. She could smell early mums, the spice of them mixing with the fragrance of the late-summer roses.

She'd studied architecture for a time, and she'd seen firsthand the majestic cathedrals in France, the romantic villas of Italy, the ancient and glorious ruins of Greece.

But this three-story building of native stone and wood, with its neat chimneys and sparkling glass, touched her as deeply as her first sight of the spires of Notre Dame.

It was, after all, haunted.

She wished she could feel it, wished some part of her was open to the shadows and whispers of the restless dead. She believed. Her dedication to science had taught her that there was much that was unexplained in the world. And as a scientist, whenever she heard of some unexplained phenomenon, she needed to know what, how, when. Who had seen it, felt it, heard it. And whether she could see, feel, hear.

It was like that with the old Barlow house, now the MacKade Inn. If she hadn't heard the stories, didn't trust Regan implicitly, Rebecca would have merely seen a beautiful house, an inviting one, with its long double porches and delightful gardens. She would have wondered how it was furnished inside, what view she might have from the windows. She might have pondered a bit over who had lived there, what they had been, where they had gone.

But she knew all that already. She had spent a great deal of time researching the original owners and their descendants.

Now she was here, walking toward that inviting porch with Regan beside her. And her heart drummed in her breast.

"It's really beautiful, Regan."

"You should have seen it before." Regan scanned the house, the land, with pride. "Poor old place, falling apart, broken windows, sagging porches. And inside . . ." She shook her head. "I have to say, even though he is my husband, Rafe has a real talent for seeing what could be, then making it happen."

"He didn't do it alone."

"No." Her lips curved as she reached for the door. "I did one hell of a job." She opened the door. "See for yourself."

One hell of a job, Rebecca thought. Beautiful wide planked floors gleamed gold with polish and sunlight. Silk-covered walls, elegantly trimmed. Antiques, both delicate and majestic, were placed in a perfect harmony that looked too natural to have been planned.

She turned into the doorway of the front parlor, with its curvy double-backed settee and Adam fireplace. Atop its carved pine mantel were gorgeous twin vases holding tall spires of larkspur and freesia and flanking silver-framed tintypes.

"You expect to hear the swish of hooped skirts," Rebecca murmured.

"That was the idea. All of the furnishings, all of the color schemes, are from the Civil War era. Even the bathrooms and kitchen reflect the feeling—even if they are modernized for comfort and convenience."

"You must have worked like fiends."

"I guess we did," Regan said reflectively. "Mostly it didn't seem like work at all. That's the way it is, I suppose, when you're dazzled by that first explosion of love."

"Explosion?" Rebecca smiled as she turned back. "Sounds scary—and violent."

"It was. There's very little calm before or after the storm when you're dealing with a MacKade."

"And apparently that's just the way you like it."

"Apparently it is. Who'd have thought?"

"Well, to tell you the truth, I always imagined you'd end up with some sophisticated, streamlined sort of man who played squash to keep in shape. Glad I was wrong."

"So am I," Regan said heartily, then shook her head. "Squash?"

"Or polo. Maybe a rousing game of tennis." Rebecca's laugh gurgled out. "Well, Regan, you were always so...tidy and chic." She lifted a brow and gestured to indicate the knife pleat in Regan's navy trousers, the polished buttons on the double-breasted blazer. "Still are."

"I'm sure you mean that in the most flattering way," Regan said dryly.

"Absolutely. I used to think, if I could just wear the kind of clothes you did—do—get my hair to swing just that way, I wouldn't feel like such a nerd."

"You were not a nerd."

"I could have given lessons in the art. But—" she ran a hand down the side of her unconstructed jacket "—I'm learning to disguise it."

"I thought I heard voices."

Rebecca looked toward the stairs and saw a small, slim blonde with a baby snuggled into a sack strapped over her breasts. Rebecca's first impression was of quiet competence. Perhaps it was the hands, she mused, one lying neatly on the polished rail, the other gently cupping the baby's bottom.

"I wondered if you were upstairs." Regan walked over to get a peek at the sleeping baby. "Cassie, you've been changing linens with the baby again."

"I like to get it done early. And Ally was fussy. This must be your friend."

"Rebecca Knight, girl genius," Regan said, with an affection that made Rebecca grin, rather than wince. "Cassandra MacKade, irreplaceable manager of the MacKade Inn."

"I'm so glad to meet you." Cassie took her hand off the rail to offer it.

"I've been looking forward to coming here for weeks. This must be quite a job, managing all this."

"It hardly ever feels like one. You'll want to look around."

"I'm dying to."

"I'll just finish upstairs. Give me a call if you need anything. There's coffee fresh in the kitchen, and muffins."

"Of course there is." Regan laughed and brushed a hand over Ally's dark hair. "Take a break, Cassie, and join the tour. Rebecca wants stories."

"Well..." Cassie glanced upstairs, obviously worrying over unmade beds.

"I'd really appreciate it," Rebecca put in. "Regan tells me you've had some experiences I'd be interested in hearing about. You actually saw a ghost."

"I..." Cassie flushed. It wasn't something she told many people about—not because it was odd, but because it was intimate.

"I'm hoping to document and record episodes while I'm here," Rebecca said, prompting her.

"Yes, Regan told me." So Cassie took a deep breath. "I saw the man Abigail Barlow was in love with. He spoke to me."

Fascinating, was all Rebecca could think as they wandered through the inn, with Cassie telling her story in a calm, quiet voice. She learned of heartbreak and murder, love lost and lives ruined. She felt chills bubble along her skin at the descriptions of spirits wandering. But she felt no deep stirring of connectedness. An interest, yes, and a full-blooded curiosity, but no sense of intimacy. She'd hoped for it.

She could admit to herself later, as she wandered alone toward the woods, that she had hoped for a personal experience, a viewing or at least a sensing of some unexplainable phenomenon. Her interest in the paranormal had grown over the years, along with her frustration at having no intimate touch with it. Except in dreams—and Rebecca knew they were merely the work of the subconscious, sometimes fraught with symbolism, sometimes as simple as a thought—she'd never been touched by the otherworldly.

Though the house had unquestionably been lovely, though it had brought back echoes of a lost past, she had seen only the beauty of it. Whatever walked there had not spoken to her.

She still had hope. Her equipment would be in by the end of the day, and Cassie had assured her she was welcome to set up in a bedroom, at least for a few days. As the anniversary of the battle drew nearer, the inn would be full with reservations already booked.

But she had some time.

When she stepped into the woods, Rebecca felt a chill, but it was only from the thick shade. Here, she knew, two young boys had fought, essentially killing each other. Others had sensed their lingering presence, heard the clash of bayonets, the cries of pain and shock. But she didn't.

She heard the call of birds, the rustle of squirrels scrambling for nuts to hoard, the faint buzz of insects. The day was too still for the air to stir the leaves, and the leaves themselves were a deep green, not even hinting of the autumn that would come within a month.

Following Cassie's competent directions, she found the stand of rocks where the two corporals were reputed to have met. Sitting down on one, she took out her notebook and began to write what she would transpose onto a computer disk later.

There have been only mild, and perhaps self-induced, sensations of déjà vu. Nothing that equals that one swift and stunning emotion at seeing the edge of the MacKade farm from the road. It's wonderful seeing Regan again, being able to view firsthand her happiness, her family. I think it must be true that there is indeed the perfect mate for some people. Regan has certainly found hers in Rafe MacKade. There's a sense of strength, of self, an arrogance, an underlying potential for physical action, in him that's oddly appealing, particularly, I would think, to a female. Offsetting it, perhaps enhancing it, is his obvious love and devotion to his wife and his children. They've made a good life, and the inn they have created is successful due to their vision. Its location and history, of course, add to its success. Undoubtedly their choice of chatelaine was also inspired.

I found Cassie MacKade to be competent, organized, and anything but aloof. There's a . . . I want to say innocence about her. Yet she is a grown woman with three children, a demanding job and, from what Regan has related to me, a miserable past. Perhaps sweetness is more accurate. In any case, I liked her immediately and felt very much at ease with her. This ease isn't something that I feel with a great many people.

I'm looking forward to meeting Devin MacKade, her husband, who is also the sheriff of Antietam. It will be interesting to see how much he resembles his brothers, not only physically, but in that less tangible but equally strong aspect of personality.

Shane MacKade has a personality that is impossible to forget. That arrogance again, though he is perhaps a bit more good-natured than his older brother, Rafe. I would theorize that Shane is a man who has great success with women. Not only due to his unquestionably stunning looks, but there's also a high degree of charm—and a blatant sexuality. Is it an earthiness, I wonder? And if so, is it due to his choice of profession?

I found myself attracted in an immediate way I'd not experienced before. All in all, it wasn't an unpleasant sensation, but one I believe it would be wise to keep to myself. I don't think a man like Shane needs any sort of encouragement.

Rebecca stopped, frowned, shook her head. Her notes, she thought with some amusement, were anything but scientific. Then again, she mused, this was more a personal journal of a personal odyssey.

In any case, I experienced nothing out of the ordinary during my tour of the MacKade Inn. Cassie and Regan showed me the bridal suite, which had once been Abigail Barlow's room, a room where she had lived in virtual seclusion the last years of her life. A room where she had died, in Cassie's opinion, by her own hand, out of despair. I walked through the master's room, Charles Barlow's room, into the nursery that is now a charming bedroom and sitting area. I explored the library, where both Regan and Cassie claim to have had strong experiences of a paranormal nature. I don't doubt their word, I merely envy their openness to such things.

It seems that despite my efforts to the contrary, I remain too rooted in the rational. Here, in woods that have been haunted for more than a century, I feel only the cool shade, see only the trees and rocks. Perhaps technology will help me. I'll see when my equipment arrives. In the meantime, I have an urge to see the MacKade farm. I'm not sure of my welcome. My impression was that Shane is as closed-minded about the paranormal as I am determined to experience it. But welcome or not, I'll cut through the woods as Cassie instructed me. If nothing else, it will be interesting to see the ins and outs of a working farm firsthand.

And, on a personal note, it won't be a hardship to get another close-up look at the farmer. He is quite beautiful.

Smiling to herself, Rebecca folded her notebook, slipped it back in her shoulder bag. She thought Shane would probably enjoy being called beautiful. She imagined he was used to it.

Her first glimpse of the farmhouse came across a fallow field that smelled strongly of manure. She didn't mind the scent, in fact it intrigued her. But she was careful to watch where she walked.

It was a peaceful scene—blue sky, puffy, harmless clouds, an old spreading willow gracefully draped near a narrow creek. At least she assumed there was a creek to her right, as the sound of gurgling water came across clearly. She saw stands of corn, row after row spearing up to the sun. Fields of grain going gold. There was a big weathered barn with those odd windows that looked like eyes, and a pale blue tower she assumed was a silo.

More silos, sheds, paddocks and pens. Cows, she thought with the ridiculous grin of the urbanite at the sight of them grazing in a green field with rocks scattered gray throughout the pasture.

From a distance it was a postcard, a quiet and remote rural scene that looked as though it were always just so. And the house, she thought, at the core of it.

Her heart was beating fast and sharply before she realized it. She stopped where she was, breathing carefully as she studied the house.

It was stone, probably from the same quarry as the inn. In this building the stone looked less elegant, more sturdy and simple. The windows were boxy and plain in the two-story structure, and the wide rear porch was a faded gray wood. She wondered if there was a front porch, and assumed there was. There would be a rocker on it, perhaps two. There would be an overhang for shade and to keep the rain off during a storm so that you could sit out and watch the clouds roll in.

Through a buzzing in her head, she heard the barking of dogs, but it barely registered. She studied the chimneys, then the gray shutters that she was sure were functional, rather than merely decorative. She could almost picture herself reaching out, drawing them in to secure the house against the night's chill— stoking the kitchen fire so that there would still be embers in the morning.

For a moment, the house was so clear, almost stark in its lines and colors against the sky, it might have been a photograph. Then she blinked and let out the breath she hadn't been aware she was holding.

That was it, of course, she realized. A photograph. Regan had described the farm to her, given her such a detailed picture of it, Rebecca decided it was her own memory of that, and her ability to project and retain, that made it all so familiar. So eerily familiar.

She laughed at herself and continued to walk, hesitating only briefly when two large yellow dogs bounded toward her. Regan had told her Shane had dogs, the parents of Regan's golden retriever. Rebecca didn't mind animals. Actually, she rather liked them, in a distant sort of way. But, obviously, these dogs had no intention of keeping their distance. They raced around her, barking, tongues lolling, tails batting back and forth in a flurry of fur.

"Nice dogs." At least she hoped they were and held out a testing hand. When her fingers were sniffed, then licked lavishly, rather than taken off at the knuckle, she relaxed. "Nice dogs," she repeated more firmly, and drummed up the nerve to rub each yellow head. "Nice, big dogs. Fred and Ethel, right?"

In agreement, each dog gave a throaty bark and raced back toward the house. Taking that as an invitation, Rebecca followed.

Pigs, she thought, and stopped by the pen to study them clinically. They weren't nearly as sloppy as she'd imagined. But they were certainly larger than she'd imagined a pig to be. When they grunted and snorted and crowded near the fence where she stood, she grinned. She was bending down to stick a hand through the slats of the fence to test the texture of pig hide when a voice stopped her.

"They'll bite."

Her hand snapped back out like a rocket. There was Shane, standing two yards away, carrying a very large wrench. Her mind went utterly blank. It wasn't fear, though he did look dangerous. It was, she would realize later, absolute sexual shock.

There were smears of grease on his arms, arms that gleamed with sweat and rippled with muscle. Arms, she thought dazedly, that were stunningly naked. He wore a thin tank-style undershirt that had probably once been white. It was a dull, washed-out gray now, snug, ripped and tucked into low-slung jeans that were worn white at the knees. He had a blue bandanna wrapped around his forehead as a sweatband, with all that wonderful black hair curling over it in a glorious tangle.

And he was smiling. A smile, Rebecca was sure, that reflected an easy knowledge of his effect on the female system.

"Bite," she repeated, fighting off the erotic cloud that covered her like fine rain.

"That's right, sweetie." He tucked the wrench into his back pocket as he walked to her. She looked so cute, he thought, standing there in her shapeless jacket, those gold eyes squinting against the sun. "They're greedy. If you don't have food in your hand when you stick it in, they'll make do with your fingers." Casually he took her hand in his, examined her fingers one by one. "Nice fingers, too. Long and slim."

"Yours are dirty." She was amazed the words didn't come out in a croak.

"I've been working."

"So I see." She managed a friendly smile as she drew her hand free. "I don't mean to interrupt."

"It's all right." He ruffled the dogs, who had come back to join the company. "The rake needed some adjustment, that's all."

Her brows shot up. "You get that dirty fixing a rake?"

His dimple flashed. "I'm not talking about a stick with tines on the end, city girl. Been over to the inn?"

"Yes. I met Cassie. She showed me through. She's going to give me a lift back to Regan's when I'm ready. Since I was in the neighborhood..." She trailed off and looked back into the pen. "I've never seen pigs close up. I wondered what they felt like."

"Mostly they feel like eating." Then he smiled again. "They're bristly," he told her. "Like a stiff brush. Not very pettable."

"Oh." She would have liked to see for herself, but wanted to keep her fingers just as they were. Instead, she turned around and took a long scan of the farm. "It's quite a place. Why haven't you planted anything over there?"

"Land needs to rest for a season now and again." He glanced toward the fallow field near the woods. "You don't really want a lecture on crop rotation, do you?"

"Maybe." She smiled. "But not right now."

"So..." He laid a hand on the fence beside her. A standard flirtation ploy, Rebecca thought, and told herself she was above such maneuvers. "What *do* you want?"

"A look around. If I wouldn't be in your way."
Instinct urged her to hunch her shoulders, shift away,
but she kept her chin up and her eyes on his.

"Pretty women aren't ever in the way." He took off
the bandanna, used it to wipe his hands before stick-
ing it in his pocket. "Come on."

Before she could evade, or think to, he had her
hand in his. The texture of his palm registered. Hard,
rough with calluses, strong. As they skirted around a
shed, she had a glimpse of a large, dangerous-looking
piece of machinery with wicked teeth.

"That's a rake," he said mildly.

"What were you doing to it?"

"Fixing it."

He headed toward the barn. Most city people, he
knew, wanted to see a barn. But when they passed the
chicken coop, she stopped.

"You raise chickens, too. For eggs?"

"For eggs, sure. And for eating."

Her skin went faintly green. "You eat your own
chickens?"

"Sweetie, at least I know what goes into my own.
Why would I pick up a pack of chicken parts at the
market?"

She made some sound and looked back over her
shoulder, toward the pigpen. Reading her perfectly,
Shane grinned. "Want to stay for dinner?"

"No, thank you," she said faintly.

He just couldn't help himself. "Ever been to a hog
butchering? It's quite an event. Real social. We usually hold one out here once a year, hook it up with a
fund-raiser for the fire department. Hog butchering
and all-you-can-eat pancake breakfast."

She pressed a hand to her unsteady stomach. "You're making that up."

"Nope. You haven't tasted sausage until—"

"I'm thinking about becoming a vegetarian," she said quickly, but pulled herself together. "That was nicely done, farm boy."

"It was a little too hard to resist." Appreciating her quick recovery, he gave her hand a quick squeeze. "You had this look in your eyes like you were calculating every squeal and cluck, filing it away somewhere for a report on the average American farm."

"Maybe I was." She shielded her eyes with the flat of her hand so that she could study his face. He really was a most remarkable-looking male. "Details interest me. So do reports. Enough details, and you have a report. A good report equals a clear picture."

"Seems to me somebody who's into details, reports and clear pictures wouldn't be out chasing ghosts."

"If scientists hadn't been interested in explaining the unknown, you'd still be working your land with a stone ax and offering sacrifices to the sun god."

With that she stepped into the barn. Stalls and concrete floors that sloped. Hay, motes of dust that tickled the nose. The light was dimmer here, and the scent of animal stronger.

Rebecca strolled toward the stalls, then let out a shriek as an enormous bovine head poked over a door and mooed at her.

"She's got an infection," Shane said, and wisely disguised a chuckle with a cough. "Had to separate her from the rest of the stock."

Rebecca's heart was slowly making its way from her throat back down to its proper place. "Oh. She's huge."

"Actually, she's on the small side. You can touch her. Here, top of the head." Taking Rebecca's reluctant hand, he held it between his and the cow. Rebecca was hard-pressed to decide which texture was tougher.

"Will she be all right?"

"Yeah, she's coming along."

"You treat the stock yourself? Don't you use a vet?"

"Not for every little thing." He liked the feel of her hand under his, the way it tensed, then slowly relaxed. The way her fingers were spread now and stroking curiously over the uninterested cow. "You don't run to the doctor every time you sneeze, do you?"

"No." She smiled, turned her head. "But I don't imagine you can find cow antibiotics at the local pharmacy."

"Feed and grain store carries most of what you need." But what he was interested in at the moment was the way she looked at him. So cool, so objective. She presented a challenge he couldn't resist. Deliberately he skimmed his gaze down to her mouth. "What do you do with all those degrees Regan says you have?"

"Collect them." With an effort, she kept her voice light. "And use them like building blocks, to get to the next."

"Why?"

"Because knowledge is power." Remembering that, and using the knowledge that he was teasing her with his easy sexuality, gave her the power to step aside. "You know, I am interested in the farm itself, and when we've got more time I hope you'll show me more of it. But what I'd really like to see now is the house and the kitchen where the young soldier died."

"We mopped up the blood a long time ago."

"That's good to hear." She cocked her head. "Is there a problem?"

Yeah, there was a problem. There were a couple of them. The first was that she was flicking him off as if he were a fly. "Regan asked me to cooperate, so I will. For her. But I don't much care for the idea of you poking around my house looking for ghosts."

"Certainly you're not afraid of what I might find."

"I'm not afraid of anything." She'd touched a nerve. A raw one. "I said I just don't like it."

"Why don't we go in, you can offer me a cold drink, and we'll see if we can come to some sort of compromise?"

It was hard to argue with reason. He took her hand again, more out of habit than in flirtation. By the time they reached the back door, he'd decided to give flirtation another shot. She smelled damn good, for a scientist.

He'd never kissed a scientist, he mused. Unless you counted Bess Trulane, the dental hygienist. He had a feeling that cool, sarcastic mouth of Rebecca's would be quite tasty.

"Got some iced tea," he offered.

"Great." It was all she said as she stood just inside the door, looking around with dark, seeking eyes.

Something. She was sure there was something here, some sensation just out of reach, blocked, she thought, by that almost overpowering male aura

Shane exuded. It clouded things, she thought, annoyed. It certainly clouded the brain.

But there was something here, amid the scrubbed tiles, the spotless counters, the old but sparkling appliances.

It was a good-size kitchen, homey with its glass-fronted cupboards showing the everyday dishes. What she imagined one would call a family kitchen— plenty of elbow room, big wooden table, sturdy chairs with cane seats. The morning paper was still on the table, where he had left it, she supposed, after reading it with his morning coffee.

There were little pots of green plants on the windowsill. She recognized them by scent, as well as sight. Rosemary, basil, thyme. The man grew herbs in his kitchen. It would have made her smile, if she hadn't been trying to get beyond him into what the room held for her.

Shane held two glasses filled with golden tea as he frowned at her. Those eyes of hers were sharp, as alert as a doe's. And her shoulders, under that oversize jacket, were stiff as boards. It made him nervous, and just a little angry, that she was studying his things and seeing something that he didn't.

''Never seen a kitchen before?''

Pasting a cool smile on her face, she turned to him. She needed to be alone here, she decided. A few minutes alone, and maybe she would get beyond that block. ''It's amazingly sexist of me, but I didn't expect to find it so tidy and organized. You know, the cheerful bachelor, living alone, entertaining willing women and poker buddies.''

This time he lifted a brow. ''I don't usually entertain them at the same time.'' He handed her the glass.

"My mother was pretty fierce about keeping the kitchen clean. You eat here, you cook here. It's like making sure the milk house is sanitized."

"The milk house." It had a charming sound to it. "I'd like to see that next time."

"Come by about 6:00 a.m., you can see it in operation. Don't you want to take off that jacket? It's warm." And he wanted to see what was under it.

"I'm fine." She moved to the back window. "Lovely view. All the windows I've looked out of since I've been here have lovely views. Do you get immune to them?"

"No. You get proprietary." To please himself, he skimmed a finger over the back of her neck. She went as still as a stone. "You've got pretty hair, Rebecca. At least, what there is of it. Of course, chopped off like this, it shows the line of your neck, and it's a nice neck. Long and white and smooth."

She recited a chunk of the periodic table in her head, so that she was calm when she turned to him. Thinking it a defense rather than a challenge, she cocked a brow, and her lips curved into an amused smile.

"Are you hitting on me, farm boy?"

Damned if he didn't want a piece of her, he realized with more than a little irritation. He particularly wanted that piece that made her voice so cool and smug.

"I've got a curiosity." He set his glass on the counter behind her, then took hers and placed it beside his. In a smooth, well-practiced move, he caged her in. "Don't you?"

"Scientists are innately curious."

He could smell her now, clean, clear soap and a hint of citrus. "How about an experiment?"

She refused to fumble, to stammer, to let him see even for an instant that she was in way, way over her head. "Of what sort?"

"Well, I do this..."

Chapter Four

He circled her waist with his hands—a surprisingly small waist—then ran them up her ribs, over to skim up her back. The punch of arousal wasn't particularly surprising. He'd certainly felt it before. But he hadn't expected quite the force of this, not with her.

Still, he enjoyed it, slid comfortably into it. When she didn't object, in fact didn't move a muscle, he aligned his body to hers until he felt her curves—not much in the way of curves—meet the angles of his.

Suddenly he really wanted to kiss her, to have a good, solid taste of that mouth. Not simply because it was female and thus desirable, but because it was Rebecca's and set in firm, almost disapproving lines.

He enjoyed being disapproved of.

But when he started to lower his head, she lifted her chin, just enough to put him off-balance.

"An experiment? What's your hypothesis?"

"Huh?"

"Your hypothesis," she repeated, relieved to have interrupted him. She'd have time enough to brace now, she decided. Time to prepare herself. "Your theory as to the outcome of your experiment."

"Theory, huh?" He kept his eyes on her mouth. It was a truly fascinating pair of lips, if a man took the time to really look at them. "How about mutual enjoyment? Is that good enough, Doc?"

"Sure." She was careful not to gulp. It would have been embarrassing, and certainly would have ruined her attempt at cool sophistication. "Why not? You want to kiss me, farm boy. Go ahead."

"I was going to." But he bypassed her mouth, just for a moment, and closed his teeth lightly over her jaw. She had the cutest little pointed chin.

Then he touched his lips to hers, just a whisper. He always liked to draw the pleasure out, for himself and the woman involved. He nibbled at them, testing their shape, their softness, and found them delightfully full, delightfully moist and giving.

Perhaps that was why he stopped thinking long enough to lose himself, to sink into that soft, wet mouth. To trace it with his tongue, tease her cool lips apart and explore.

Dark and deep was her taste, yet oddly familiar. He wondered how it could be that he was kissing her for the first time, yet he could be sure, deadly sure, that he had experienced her taste before. And the familiarity was impossibly exciting, desperately arousing.

She was so tiny. Taut little muscles, slim back, small, firm breasts yielding erotically against him. And the flavor of her, a cool, damp meadow, a quiet, shadowy glade, stirred his blood. Stirred it so that several dizzy minutes passed before he realized she hadn't moved. She wasn't touching him, her lips weren't sliding under his. She had made not one single sound.

The absolute absence of response was as effective as a slap. He stepped back, the first movement jerky before he could get a hold of himself. With his brows drawn together hard, he studied her passive face, the faintly interested eyes, the amused quirk of that luscious mouth.

"That was very nice," she said, in a tone so mild he nearly snarled. "Was that your best shot?"

He only stared at her, his gorgeous sea-toned eyes molten. He could handle rejection. A woman had every right to reject a man's advances. But he wouldn't tolerate snickering. And, damn it, he knew she was snickering under that placid exterior.

To keep from humiliating himself further, he latched tight to control. Without it, he would have hauled her into his arms again and loosed some of the hot, violent passion she'd managed to incite in him without the least effort.

"Let's just say, as experiments go, that one was a dud. I've got work to do." With some dignity, he nodded toward the wall phone. "Go ahead and give Cass a call whenever you're done here."

"Thanks. See you tonight at dinner."

At the door, he turned, glared at her. She continued to stand there, leaning back against the counter. Her pretty cap of hair wasn't even mussed.

"You're a cool one, Rebecca."

"So I'm told. Thanks for the drink, farm boy. And the experiment."

The moment the door slammed behind him, she sagged against the counter. She wanted to sit, but was very much afraid her legs would buckle before she managed to cross the three feet of tile to a chair.

She'd never known that anyone, anywhere, could kiss like that.

Her head was still reeling. Now that she was alone, she pressed a hand to her jumping heart and took several long, deep breaths that echoed in the room like those of a diver hitting the surface. That was apt, she supposed. She felt as though she'd been dragged into some deep, dark, airless space and escaped just in the nick of time.

Obviously, the man was a danger to female society. No woman could be safe around him.

She picked up her drink, watched the ice cubes clink musically together as she brought it to her assaulted lips with a shaky hand.

But she'd held together, she reminded herself. Held herself aloof and distant by desperately reciting Henry V's St. Crispin's Day speech. God knew where that had come from, but it had kept her from whimpering like a starving puppy. True, she'd begun to lose her concentration by the time she reached "We few, we happy few," but then Shane had ended it.

If he'd kept it up for another ten seconds, she'd never have finished the speech, unless it was in incoherent mewings.

"Oh, boy," she managed now, and downed every drop in the glass. The chilly tea cooled the heat in her throat, if not in her blood.

This kind of passion was a new experience. She imagined Shane MacKade would hoot in unholy amusement if he knew just how violently he'd affected her. Her. Dr. Rebecca Knight, professional genius, perennial virgin.

She could congratulate herself that she'd maintained her composure, that she'd maintained at least the appearance of composure while the top of her head was spinning around a good six inches above her cranium. If he had even a hint of her stupidity in the ways of men and women, the slightest clue of her dazzled reaction to him personally, he would certainly press his advantage.

Not only would she get nothing done during her stay, she was dead certain she would leave with a bruised heart.

She was sure wiser women than she had fallen hard for the charm of Shane MacKade. That kind of chemistry could only result in fiery explosions. The safest position was to keep herself aloof, to annoy him if and when it was necessary, and never to let him know she was attracted.

Safe, Rebecca thought with a sigh as she set her empty glass in the sink. She had good reason to know just how tedious safety could be. But she had come to Antietam to prove something to herself. To explore possibilities and to add to her reputation.

Shane wasn't a part of the plan.

His house was, however. She drew another deep breath, tried to settle her jolted nerves. There was something here for her, she was sure of it. She couldn't feel it now, not when her system was sparkling like hot, naked wires.

She would have to come back, she decided. She would have to come back and make sure she had time to explore the possibilities here. The only way to manage that, she decided, was to simultaneously charm Shane and keep him at arm's length.

Dinner at Regan's would be a good start.

It seemed to Rebecca that there were children everywhere—babies, toddlers, older kids, all going about the business of cooing, squabbling, racing. Toys were spread all over the living room rug, where Regan's Nate could compete with his cousin Layla for the best and brightest building block.

She knew who belonged to whom now. Layla, who held her own with her slightly older cousin, belonged to Jared and Savannah, as did the slim, dark-haired boy, Bryan. She knew Jared was the oldest of the MacKade brothers, a lawyer who seemed very at home in his loosened tie.

His wife was quite possibly the most stunning woman Rebecca had ever seen. Hugely pregnant, her thick, black hair twisted back in a braid, dark eyes sultry and amused, Savannah looked, to Rebecca's mind, like some well-satisfied fertility goddess.

Connor was about Bryan's age, as fair as his cousin was dark, and with Cassie's slow shy warmth in his eyes. There was Emma, a golden pixie of about seven, who squeezed into the chair beside her stepfather. Rebecca found it both sweet and telling to see the easy way Devin MacKade's arm curled around the little girl while he held his sleeping baby in the crook of the other.

Wild and tough the MacKade brothers might be, but Rebecca had never seen any men so deeply entrenched in family.

"So, what do you think of Antietam so far?" Rafe stepped expertly over dog, toys and children to top off Rebecca's glass of wine.

"I think a lot of it," she said, and flashed him a quick smile. "It's charming, quiet, bursting with history."

He cocked a brow. "Haunted?"

"No one seems to doubt it." She cast an amused look at Shane, who'd settled down next to Savannah to pat her belly. "Almost no one."

"Some people block their imagination." Casually Savannah shifted Shane's hand to the left, where the baby was kicking vigorously. "There are some places in this area with very strong memories."

It was an intriguing way of putting it, Rebecca mused. "Memories."

Savannah shrugged. "Violent death, and violent unhappiness, leave marks, deep ones. Of course, that's not very scientific."

"That would depend on what theory you subscribe to," Rebecca answered.

"I guess we've all had some experience with the ghosts, or leftover energy, or whatever you choose to call it," Jared began.

"Speak for yourself." Shane tipped back his beer. "I don't go around talking to people who aren't there."

Jared only grinned. "He's still ticked off about when I scared the hell out of him when we were kids, spending the night in the old Barlow place."

Recognizing the look in Shane's eye, Devin decided to step in as peacemaker. "Scared the hell out of all of us," he said. "Rattling chains, creaking boards. I imagine you're looking for something a little more subtle, Rebecca.''

''Well, I'm certainly looking.'' It surprised and pleased her when Nate toddled over and crawled into her lap. She hadn't been around children enough to know whether she appealed to them, or they to her. ''I'm anxious to get started,'' she added as Nate toyed with the tourmaline pendant she wore.

''Dinner in five,'' Regan announced, her face prettily flushed, as she hurried in from the kitchen. ''Let's round up these kids. Rafe?''

''Jason's asleep. I already put him down.''

''I'll get Layla.'' Shane shot Savannah a wicked grin. ''It's going to take Jared at least five minutes to haul you up from the couch.''

''Jared, make sure you punch him after we eat.''

''Done,'' Jared assured his wife, and rose to help her up.

As exits went, it was a noisy one, as was the meal that followed. The big dining room, with its tall windows, held them all comfortably, the long cherry-wood table generous enough to make room for the necessary high chairs.

The choice of spaghetti with marinara sauce, platters of antipasto and crusty bread was, Rebecca thought, inspired. There was enough for an army, and the troops dug in.

She wasn't used to family meals, to spilled milk, scattershot conversations, arguments, or the general, friendly mess of it all. It made her feel like an observer again, but not unhappily so. A new experience, she thought, one to be enjoyed, as well as assessed.

She found it oddly stimulating that, while not everyone talked about the same things, they usually talked at the same time. Both toddlers smeared sauce lavishly on themselves and over their trays. More than once during the meal, she felt the warm brush of fur against her legs as the dog searched hopefully for dropped noodles or handouts.

She couldn't quite keep up as conversations veered from baseball to the late-summer harvest, from teething to town gossip, with a variety of unconnected subjects in between.

It dazzled her.

Her memories of family dinners were of quiet, structured affairs. One topic of conversation was introduced and discussed calmly and in depth for the course of the meal, and the meal would last precisely one hour. Like a class, Rebecca mused now. A well-organized, well-constructed and well-ordered class—at the end of which she would be firmly dismissed to attend to her other studies.

As the careless confusion swirled around her, she found herself miserably unhappy with the memory.

"Eat."

"What?" Distracted, she turned her head and found a forkful of pasta at her lips. Automatically she opened her mouth and accepted it.

"That was easy." Shane rolled another forkful, held it out. "Try again."

"I can feed myself, thanks." Struggling with embarrassment, she scooped up spaghetti.

"You weren't," he pointed out. "You were too busy looking around like you'd just landed on an alien planet." He reached for the wine bottle and topped off her glass before she could stop him. She never drank more than two glasses in an evening. "Is that what the MacKades look like, from a scientific viewpoint?"

"They look interesting," she said coolly. "From any viewpoint. How does it feel to be a member of such a dynamic family?"

"Never thought about it."

"Everyone thinks of family, where they come from, how they fit in, or don't."

"It's just the way it is." Shane helped himself to another generous serving from the communal pot.

"But, as the youngest, you'd—"

"Are you analyzing me, Doc? Don't we need a couch and a fifty-minute clock?"

"I'm just making conversation." Somehow, she realized, she'd gotten out of rhythm. And she'd been doing so well. She made an effort to settle herself, took a slow sip of wine. "Why don't you tell me about this hay you're going to mow?"

He angled his head. He knew when a woman was yanking his chain, and he knew how to tug back. "I'll have the mower out tomorrow. You can come on by and see for yourself. Maybe lend a hand. I can always use an extra pair of arms—even skinny ones."

"That sounds fascinating, but I'm going to be busy. My equipment came in." She twirled her fork and neatly nipped pasta from the tines. "But later on, when I set up at your place, I'm sure I can find the time now and then to help you out. In fact, I'm looking forward to observing you in your natural milieu."

"Is that right?" He shifted, turning to face her. The hand he rested on the back of her chair brushed her shoulder on the way. And her quick, involuntary jolt did a great deal to smooth out his ego, which was still raw from their earlier encounter.

Deliberately he leaned closer, just a little closer. "If that's what you want, Rebecca, why don't you come on home with me tonight? We'll—"

"Shane, stop flirting with Rebecca." Regan shook her head as she looked down the table. "You're embarrassing her."

"I wasn't flirting. We were having a conversation." His lips curved, his dimple winked. "Weren't we, Rebecca?"

"Of sorts."

"Shane can't keep his eyes, or his hands, off the ladies." Too logy and sluggish to do justice to the meal, Savannah pushed back her half-finished plate. "The smart ones don't take him seriously."

"Good thing Rebecca's one of the smart ones," Devin put in. "I tell you, it's a sad thing to watch the way some women come sniffing around him."

"Yeah, I get real depressed about it." Shane grinned wickedly. "I can hardly hold my head up. Just last week, Louisa Tully brought me out a peach pie. It was demoralizing."

Rafe snorted. "The trouble is, too many of them haven't figured out the way to your heart isn't through your stomach. It's through your— Ow!" He winced, laughing, when Regan kicked him hard under the table. "*Mind.* I was going to say *mind.*"

"I'm sure you were," Regan said primly.

"Shane's always kissing somebody." Bryan shoveled in the last bite of his third helping, and used his napkin rather than the back of his hand to wipe his mouth only because he caught his mother's eye.

Enjoying herself now, Rebecca leaned forward to smile at the boy. "Is he really?"

"Oh, yeah. At the farm, at the ballpark, right in town, too. Some of them giggle." He rolled his eyes. "Con and I think it's disgusting."

Shane had always thought that fire was best met with fire, and he turned to his nephew. "I hear Jenny Metz is stuck on you."

Bryan flushed from his sauce-smeared chin to the roots of his hair. "She is not." But the humiliation of that, and the primal fear of girls, was enough to shut his mouth firmly.

Jared sent his stepson a sympathetic look and steered the conversation onto safer ground.

From her vantage point, Rebecca saw Shane lean over, murmur something to the hunched-shouldered Bryan that made the boy grin.

The sound of fretful crying sounded through one of the baby monitors almost as soon as the meal was over. After a heated debate, Rebecca started on the dishes. Babies needed to be tended to, as she'd pointed out. Children put to bed. She was better suited to washing dishes than to fulfilling either of those responsibilities. And—and that clinched it— was she a friend or a guest?

While she worked, she could hear voices from the living room and more sounds through the other monitor that stood in the kitchen. Some soft, some deep. Soothing, she mused. A kind of routine that dug roots, honed traditions. She could hear Rafe talking to Nate as he readied him for bed, Regan murmuring to the baby as she nursed him.

Someone—she thought it was Devin's voice—was calmly directing children to pick up the scattered toys.

Jared poked his head in once, apologizing for skipping out on kitchen duty, explaining that Savannah was exhausted.

She waved him away.

She was sure that if anyone else had to face a mess like this, the piles of pots, pans, dishes, glasses would be daunting at best, tedious at worst. But for her it was a novel chore, and therefore entertaining.

Shane strolled in, thumbs hooked in his pockets. "Looks like I'd better roll up my sleeves."

"You don't need to pitch in." Rebecca was working the problem of fitting everything into the racks of the dishwasher into a geometric equation. "I've got it."

"Everybody else is tied up with kids or pregnant wives. I'm all you've got." So he did roll up his sleeves. "Are you going to put the dishes in there, or study it all night?"

"I'm working on a system." Fairly satisfied with it, Rebecca began to load. "What are you doing?"

"I'm going to wash the pans."

She paused, her eyes narrowing a bit as she recalculated. "That would be simpler." She caught a whiff of lemon from the soap he squirted into the hot running water. But when she bent over, her bottom bumped his thigh and had her straightening again.

"Close quarters around the sink," he said with an easy grin.

To offset it, she merely walked to the other side of the dishwasher and worked from there. "So, is flirting with women a vocation or an avocation?"

"It's a pleasure."

"Mmm... Isn't it awkward, in a small town, to juggle women?"

"I guess it would be, if you thought of them as rubber balls instead of people."

She nodded as she meticulously arranged dishes. It would be, she mused, interesting and educational to delve into the mind of a ladies' man. "I'll rephrase that. Isn't it awkward to begin or end a relationship in a small town where people appear to know a great deal about other people's business?"

"Not if you do it right. Is this another study, Rebecca?"

She straightened again, battling a flush because it had been just that. "I'm sorry. Really. That's a terrible habit of mine—picking things apart. Just say, 'Butt out, Rebecca.'"

"Butt out, Rebecca."

Because there had been no sting in the order, she laughed and got back to work. "What if I just say I think you have a wonderful and interesting family, and I enjoyed meeting all of them?"

"That would be fine. I'm fond of them myself."

"It shows." She looked up, lips curved. "And it almost makes me think there's more to you than a woman-chasing farm boy. I enjoyed watching all of you together, the interaction, the shorthand conversations, the little signals."

He set a pan into the drainer. "Is that what you were doing when I caught you at dinner? Making observations on the MacKades in their natural milieu?"

Her smile faded a little. "No, actually, I was thinking of something else entirely." Suddenly restless, she picked up a damp cloth and walked away to wipe off the stove. "I do need to talk to you about making arrangements to work at the farm. I realize you have a routine, and a private life. I don't intend to get in your way."

But you will, he thought. He'd suspected it before, but that quick glimpse of sadness in her eyes moments ago had confirmed it. He was a sucker for a woman with secrets and sad stories.

"I told Regan you could come and work there, so I'm stuck with it."

She shrugged her shoulder. "It's important enough to me that I can't worry overmuch about it making you uncomfortable." When she glanced back at him, her eyes were cool again, faintly mocking. "You'll be out in the field most of the time, won't you? Baling hay, or whatever?"

"Or whatever." Damned if she wasn't pulling his strings, he thought. Both of her. For he was certain there were two women in there, and he had a growing fascination with each one.

Though he hadn't quite finished the pans, he picked up a towel, dried his hands. Maybe it was that slim white neck, he mused. It was just begging to be touched, tasted. Or it could be those odd golden eyes that hinted at all sorts of elusive emotions, even when they shone with confidence. Or maybe it was just his own ego, still ruffled from her mocking response to him that morning.

Whatever it was, he was compelled to test her, and perhaps himself, again.

He moved behind her, quietly. Following impulse, he lowered his head and closed his teeth gently on the sensitive nape of her neck. She jerked, came up hard against him with a shudder that seemed to rack her from head to toe. As surprised as he was pleased, he took her shoulders firmly in his hands and turned her to face him.

"Not so cool this time," he murmured, and crushed her mouth with a kiss of practiced skill and devastating intensity.

She hadn't had time to brace, to think, to defend. His mouth quite simply destroyed her. Her head spun, her knees jellied, her blood went on fast boil. Never in her life had so many sensations battered her at once. The smooth, warm demand of his mouth taking from hers, the hard, confident hands moving over her, the smell of lemon and soap and . . . man.

Her mind simply couldn't compute it, so her body took over. Some weak, accepting sound purred out of her throat. She couldn't stop it, couldn't stop the trembling or the heat or the sudden and baffling need to let everything she was melt into him. One shock of pleasure sparked another, then another, until there was nothing else.

His first reaction was of arrogant delight. Indifferent to him? Like hell she was. She was hot. She was trembling. She was moaning. The woman he kissed that morning had been cool and amused and mocking. Not this one. This one was . . .

Deliciously warm. He could have tasted that mouth endlessly, so smooth, so soft, so silky. He eased deeper, aroused by each throaty moan and murmur. His mind went blissfully blank with pleasure when he slid his hands under her sweater and found only Rebecca beneath it.

She quivered, her breath catching in her throat as he skimmed those rough palms over small, firm breasts. His thumbs scraped lightly over her rigid nipples, and he swallowed her gasps, absorbed her shudders.

The arms she'd lifted to twine around his neck went limp, dropped slowly to her sides in a kind of helpless surrender that excited unbearably, even as it warned him.

He eased back, clamping his hands on the stove at either side of her as he studied her face. Her cheeks were flushed, her eyes were closed, her breath was coming fast and harsh through lips erotically swollen from his.

He thought she would look just like that on the floor, with him mounting her. The image of that had him gripping the stove until his fingers ached.

Then she opened her eyes, and he saw that they were blind, drugged, and a little bit afraid.

"Well, well, well..." He said it lightly, mockingly, as much in defense as in triumph, as his stomach lurched with need. "I'd say we had a different result this time around."

She couldn't catch her breath, much less form a word. She only shook her head as her body continued to suffer from quick, lethal explosions.

"No theories this time, Doc?" He didn't know why he was angry, but he could feel his temper building. Building, then spiking, as she stood there looking helpless, stunned, and more and more terrified. "Maybe we should try it again."

"No." She got that out. She thought her life might depend on the uttering of that single syllable. "No," she said again. "I think you proved your point."

He didn't know what his point had been—something about amusing himself, a test—but it certainly didn't apply now. Now he wanted her with a ferocity that was totally unprecedented. He believed desire was as natural as breathing, and should cause no more discomfort than the easy exhaling of air.

And yet he ached, fiercely ached.

"You... Let me by," she managed.

"When I'm ready. I'm waiting for your hypothesis—or would it be a conclusion now? I'm curious, Rebecca. How are you going to react the next time I kiss you? And which one of you am I going to find when I take you to bed?"

She didn't know—and wasn't sure she could tell him if she did. She was saved from what she was sure would have been abject humiliation when Rafe swung through the kitchen door.

He stopped, summed up the situation in a glance and scowled at his brother. "For God's sake, Shane."

"Get out."

"It's my damn house," Rafe shot back.

"Then we'll get out." He snagged Rebecca's arm and took two strides before panic gave her the strength to yank away.

"No." It was all she said as she walked past both men and out of the kitchen.

"What the hell's wrong with you?" Rafe demanded. "You had her pinned up against the damn stove. She was white as a sheet. Since when have you gotten off on scaring women?"

"I didn't scare her."

But he realized abruptly that he had, and that for a few moments he hadn't cared that he had. In fact, he been hotly thrilled that he could. That was new for him, and shaming.

"I didn't mean to. It got out of hand." Frustrated, he dragged his unsteady fingers through his hair. "Hell, I got out of hand."

"Maybe you'd better keep your distance until you can handle yourself."

"Yeah, maybe I'd better."

Because he'd been expecting an argument, Rafe's brows drew together. He noted now that Shane was just about as pale as Rebecca had been. "You okay?"

"I don't know." Baffled, Shane shook his head. "She's the damnedest woman," he muttered. "The damnedest woman."

Chapter Five

As she was a meticulous woman, it took Rebecca hours to set her equipment to her specifications. There were sensors, cameras, recorders, computers, monitors. Cassie had been able to give her one of the larger suites for a couple of days, and she tried to be grateful for it. Yet it was confining not to be able to set up a camera or two on the first floor.

She doubted any of the other guests would welcome one in the rooms they slept in.

Still, she had space, and the thrill of occupying what had been Charles Barlow's room. The windows afforded a lovely view of the sloping front lawn, the late-summer flowers, the wild tiger lilies lining the edge of the road, and the town itself. She imagined the master of the house would have enjoyed looking out, studying the rooftops and chimneys of the houses and shops, the quiet stream of traffic.

Everything she'd read about Charles Barlow indicated that he had been the kind of man who would consider it his right, even his duty, to look down on lesser men.

She wished she could feel him here, his power, even his cruelty. But there was nothing but a charming set of rooms, crowded now with the technology she'd brought with her.

It was frustrating. She was positive every one of the MacKades had experienced something in this house, had been touched by what lingered there. Why couldn't she?

Her hope was that science would aid her, as it always had. She'd purchased the very best equipment suited to a one-person operation, and shrugged off the expense. Some women, she mused, bought shoes or jewelry. She bought machines.

All right, perhaps she was buying more in the shoes-and-jewelry line these days. Money had never been a problem, and didn't look to be one in the foreseeable future. In any case, she was entitled to her hobby, Rebecca told herself as she dipped her hands in her pockets. She was entitled to the new life, the new persona she was carving out.

A great many of her colleagues thought she had gone mad when word got out on what she planned to spend her free time studying. Her parents would be deeply annoyed—if she ever drew up the courage to face them with her new interest. But she wasn't going to let that matter.

She wanted to explore. Needed to. If she had to go back to being the boring, predictable, utterly tedious Dr. Knight, she *would* go mad.

Yet she'd learned a valuable lesson the night before. She wasn't quite ready to handle certain aspects of her new life. She'd been cocky, entirely too self-assured, and Shane MacKade had knocked the chip from her shoulder and crushed it to splinters. Lord knew why she'd thought she could deal with sex.

All he'd had to do was catch her off guard once, and she'd turned into a trembling, mindless mess. She'd spent some time being furious with him for causing it—after she got over being terrified. But she was too analytical to blame him for long. She had put on the mask of confidence, had even tried her hand at flirtation. It was hardly his fault that he'd believed the image and responded to it.

She would simply have to be more careful in the future, and rethink her plan to stay at the farm. The man was entirely too physical, too attractive. Too everything. Especially for a woman who had barely begun to explore her own sexuality.

Yes, she would be very careful, and she wouldn't dwell on those sharp and intense needs he'd stirred up in her—the way his mouth had felt on hers, the way his hands had moved over her bare skin. What it had felt like to be touched that way, by that man. So intimately. So naturally.

She let out a long, shaky breath and closed her eyes.

No, she wouldn't dwell on that. She was going to enjoy herself, start her paper on Antietam, make plans for the book she intended to write. And, if perseverance counted for anything, find her ghosts.

Moving to her computer, she sat and booted up.

I'm settled in the MacKade Inn now, in what were Charles Barlow's rooms during the Civil War period. There are other guests, and I'll be interested to hear if they had any experiences during the night. For the moment, all is quiet. I'm told that people often hear doors slamming, or the sound of weeping, even the report of a gun. These phenomena happen not only at night, but also during the daylight hours.

Regan has experienced them, and Rafe. There are also reports of the scent of roses. This particular experience is most common. I find this interesting as the olfactory sense is the strongest.

In my brief meeting with Savannah MacKade, I learned that she has often felt a presence in this house, and the woods that border the land. I gather that both she and Jared are similarly drawn to the woods where the two corporals met and fought.

It's fascinating to me that people find each other this way.

Cassie and Devin MacKade are another example. In this case, they lived in the same small town all of their lives. Cassie married someone else and had two children, and from what I can glean, a truly horrific marriage. Still, she and Devin found each other, and from this outsider's perspective, seem as though they've been together always.

Both Cassie and Devin have stories to tell about the inn, and their experiences here. I'll have to go into them in depth in my official notes.

Shane MacKade is the only one who has no stories to tell—or rather none he's willing to tell. I'm not used to relying on my instincts rather than pure data, but if I were to trust them I'd say he holds back what he knows or feels. Which is contradictory, as he isn't a man who seems to hold back anything on a personal level.

I'd have to say he's one of the most demonstrative people I've even encountered. He's a habitual toucher, and by reputation one who enjoys the company of women. I suppose one would call him earthy, without the cruder connotations of the word. He is basically a man of the earth, and perhaps that explains why he scoffs at anything that hints of the paranormal.

To be honest, I like him very much. His humor, his obvious attachment to family, his unabashed love of the land. On the surface, he appears to be a simple man, yet—using those rusty instincts of mine—I sense complications underneath.

He would certainly make an interesting study.

However

"The lady doesn't come in here."

Fingers still poised on the keyboard, Rebecca glanced up and saw Emma in the doorway. "Hello. Is school out?"

"Uh-huh. Mama said to come tell you she has coffee and cookies if you want." Very much at home, Emma wandered in, gazing wide-eyed at the machines. "You have a lot of stuff."

"I know. I guess you could say they're my toys. Who's the lady?"

"She's the one who used to live here. She cries, like Mama used to. Didn't you hear her?"

"No. When?"

With calm and friendly eyes, Emma smiled. "Just now. She was crying while you were typing. But she never comes in here."

A quick, cold shiver spurted down Rebecca's spine. "You heard her, just now?"

"She cries a lot." Emma walked over to the computer and solemnly read the words on the monitor. "Sometimes I go to her room, and she stops crying. Mama says she likes company."

"I see." Rebecca was careful to keep her tone light. "And when you hear her crying, how does it make you feel?"

"It used to make me sad. But now I know sometimes crying can make you feel better when you're finished."

In spite of herself, Rebecca smiled. "That's very true."

"Are you going to take pictures of the lady?"

"I hope so. Have you ever seen her?"

"No, but I think she's pretty, because she smells pretty." Emma offered another quick, elfin smile. "You smell pretty, too."

"Thanks. Do you like living in the house, Emma, with the lady and everything?"

"It's nice. But we're going to build our own house, near the farm, because we're a big family now. Mama will still work here, so I can come whenever I want. Are you writing a story? Connor writes stories."

"No, not exactly. It's like a diary, really. Just things I want to remember, or read over sometime. But I'm going to write a story about Antietam."

"Can I be in it?"

"Oh, I think you have to be." She ran a hand over Emma's springy golden curls. It was lovely to discover that, yes, she did seem to appeal to children. And they appealed, very much, to her. "I hope you'll tell me all about the lady."

"My name's Emma MacKade now. The judge said it could be. So I'll be Emma MacKade in the story."

"You certainly will be." Rebecca shut down her machine. "Let's go get some cookies."

She hadn't intended to walk over to the farm. She'd set out to take a stroll in the woods—or so she'd told herself. To take some air, clear her mind, stretch her legs.

But she was out of the trees and crossing the fields before she knew it.

She couldn't say why it made her smile to see the house. She hoped it was late enough in the day that Shane was settled in somewhere, or off with one of his lady friends. She knew that farm work started early in the day, so it seemed safe to assume it would be done by now.

She could see that part of a hayfield had been mowed, but there was no tractor, or whatever was used to cut it, in sight now. She was sorry she'd missed the action. Undoubtedly Shane MacKade riding through the fields on a large, powerful machine would make quite an interesting picture.

But it was really solitude she wanted, before she went back to her rooms and hunkered down with her equipment and notes for the rest of the night.

That was why she veered away from the house, rather than toward it.

She liked the smells here, found them oddly familiar. Some deeply buried memory, she supposed. Perhaps a former life. She was really going to start exploring the theory of reincarnation sometime soon. Fascinating subject.

Because she knew the story of the two corporals well, she wandered toward the outbuildings. She didn't know precisely what a smokehouse might look like, but Regan had told her it was stone, and that it still stood.

There were wildflowers in the grass, little blue stars, yellow cups, tall, lacy spears of white. Charmed, she forgot her mission and began to gather a few. Beyond where she stood was a meadow, lushly green, starred with color from more wild blooms and the flutter of butterflies.

Had she ever taken time to walk in a meadow? she wondered. No, never. Her botany studies had been brief, and crowded with Latin names rather than with enjoyment.

So, she would enjoy it now. Light of heart, she walked toward the wide field of high grass, noting the way the sun slanted, the way the flowers swayed— danced, really—in the light breeze.

Then her throat began to ache, and her heartbeat thickened. For a moment there was such a terrible sadness, such a depth of loneliness, she nearly staggered. Her fingers clutched tightly at the flowers she'd picked.

She moved through the high grass, among the thistles shooting up purple puffs on thick stalks, and the sorrow clutched in her stomach like a fist. She stopped, watched butterflies flicker, listened to birds chirping. The strong sun warmed her skin, but inside she was so very cold.

What else could we have done? she asked herself, shivering with a grief that wasn't her own, yet was stunningly real. *What else was there to do?*

Opening her hand, she let the flowers fall in the meadow grass at her feet. The tears stinging her eyes left her shaken, baffled. As carefully as a soldier in a minefield, she backed away from where her flowers lay in the grass.

Done about what? she wondered, a little frantic now. Where had the question come from, and what could it possibly mean? Then she turned, taking slow, deliberate breaths, and left the meadow behind.

All those strong, confusing emotions faded so that she began to doubt she'd ever felt them. Perhaps it was just that she was a little lonely, or that it was lowering to realize she wasn't a woman to gather wildflowers or walk in meadows.

She was a creature of books and classrooms, of facts and theory. She'd been born that way. Certainly she'd been raised that way, uncompromisingly. The brilliant child of brilliant parents who had outlined and dictated her world so well, and for so long, that she was fully adult before she thought to question and rebel. Even in such a small way.

And the life she wanted to create for herself was still so foreign. Even now, she was thinking of going back, of keeping to her timetable, of sitting down with her equipment. No matter that it was something out of the ordinary that she intended to study, it was still studying.

Damn it.

Jamming her hands in her pockets, she deliberately turned away from the direction that would take her back to the inn. She would have her walk first, she ordered herself. She'd pick more wildflowers if she wanted to. Next time, she'd take off her shoes and walk in the meadow.

She was muttering to herself when she saw the cows, bumping together under a three-sided shed that was attached to the milk barn. Didn't cows belong in the fields? she wondered. There were so many of them crowded together there, munching on what she supposed was hay or alfalfa.

Curious, she walked closer, keeping some distance only because she wasn't entirely sure cows were as friendly as they looked. But when they didn't seem the least concerned with her, she moved closer.

And heard him singing.

"One for the morning glory, two for the early dew, three for the man who stands his ground and four for the love of you..."

Delighted with the sound, Rebecca moved to the doorway and had her first glimpse of a milking parlor.

Whatever she'd imagined, it wasn't this organized, oddly technical environment. There were big, shiny pipes and large chutes, the mechanical hum of a compressor or some other type of machine. A dozen cows stood in stanchions, eating contentedly from individual troughs. Some of them munched on grain as devices that looked like clever octopuses relieved them of their milk.

And Shane, stripped down to one of those undeniably sexy undershirts, a battered cap stuffed onto all that wonderful, wild hair, moved among them, still singing, or dropping into a whistle, as he checked feed or the progress of the milking machines.

"Okay, sweetie, all done."

Caught up in the process, Rebecca stepped closer. "How does that work?"

He swore ripely, bumping the cow hard enough to have her moo in annoyance. The look he aimed at Rebecca was not one of friendly welcome.

"I'm sorry. I didn't mean to sneak up on you. It's noisy." She tried a smile, and forced herself not to take a step in retreat. "I was out walking, and I saw the cows out there, and I wondered what was going on."

"The same thing that goes on around here twice a day, every day." It was an effort for him to readjust himself. He'd planned to avoid her for a few days, but here she was, pretty as a picture with those big, curious eyes, right in his milking parlor.

"But how do you manage it all by yourself? There are so many of them."

"I don't always do it alone. Anyway, it's automated, for the most part." Deftly he removed inflations from udders.

"Where does the milk go? Through the pipes, I imagine."

"That's right." He bit back a sigh. He didn't much feel like giving her a class in Milking 101. He felt like kissing the breath out of her. "From cow to pipes and into tanks in the milk house." He gestured vaguely. "It keeps it at the proper temperature until the milk truck pumps it out. I have to take these girls back to the loafing shed."

"Loafing shed?"

He did smile now, just a little. "That's where they loaf, before and after."

Rebecca made way, perhaps a bit more than necessary, as he herded the milked cows out. She wondered how he kept them straight, the ones still to be milked, the ones who had been. And when he herded more in, she realized the answer was obvious.

Their bags were huge. She muffled a giggle as he moved them into place. With approval for the efficiency and organization of the system she watched him pull a lever that poured grain from chutes to troughs.

"So they feed and milk at the same time."

"Food's the incentive." He paid little attention to her as he went about his business. "They eat, you milk half of them. You milk the other half while you set up the next group."

Quickly, and with little fuss, he hooked his new stock into their stanchions. "These are inflations. They go over the teats, do the work that used to be done by hand. You can milk a hell of a lot more cows a hell of a lot faster this way than with your fingers and a bucket."

"It must be more sanitary. And you use that solution—some sort of antiseptic, I suppose—on their..."

"Bags, honey. You call them bags." He nodded. "You want grade A milk, you have to meet the standards."

"How is the milk graded?" she began, then stopped herself. "Sorry. Too many questions. I'm in your way."

"Yeah, you are." But, as the machines did their work, he stepped toward her. "What are you doing here, Rebecca?"

"I told you, I was out walking."

He lifted a brow, hooked his thumbs in his front pockets. "And you decided to visit with the cows?"

"I didn't have a plan."

"I think it's safe to say you usually do."

"All right." He was, of course, on target, no matter what she'd told herself when she started through the woods. "I suppose I felt we'd left something unresolved. I don't want things to be difficult with you, since I'm dealing with so much of your family while I'm here."

"Um-hmm…" He wasn't precisely sure which side of her he was dealing with at the moment. "I was pushy. Do you want an apology?"

"Unnecessary."

That made him smile again. He had a growing affection for that cocky tilt to her chin. "Want to try it again? I've got an urge to kiss you right now."

"I'm sure you have an urge to kiss any woman, just about anytime."

"Yeah. But you're here."

"I'll let you know if and when I want you to kiss me." As a means of defense, she turned, wandered, frowned intently at a container labeled Udder Balm. "The problem I have is that as long as we have this…"

"Attraction?" he put in. "Lust?"

"Tension," she snapped back. "It makes it difficult for me to follow through on my plan to work here. I do want to work here," she said, turning to him again. "But I can't if I'm going to have to deflect unsolicited advances."

"Unsolicited advances." Instead of being annoyed, he nearly doubled over with laughter. "Damn,

Rebecca, I love the way you talk when you're being snotty. Say something else.''

"I'm sure you're more used to women keeling over at your feet," she said coldly. "Or bringing you peach pies. I just want to be certain that you clearly understand the word *no.*"

He didn't find anything amusing about that. She had the fascinating experience of watching his grin turn into a snarl. "You said no last night, didn't you?"

"My point is—"

"I could have had you, right there on my brother's kitchen floor."

The color that temper had brought to her cheeks faded away, but her voice remained steady and cool. "You overestimate your appeal, farm boy."

"Watch your step, Becky," he said quietly. "I've got a mean streak. You want to dissolve some tension so you can get on with your project. I've always found honesty goes a long way to cutting the tension. You wanted me every bit as much as I wanted you. Maybe you were surprised. Maybe I was, too, but that's the fact."

She opened her mouth, but found no suitable lies tripping onto her tongue. "All right. I won't deny I was interested for a moment."

"Honey, what you were was a long way up from interested."

"Don't tell me what I felt, or what I feel. I will tell you that if you think I'm going to be another notch on your bedpost, think again."

"Fine." In casual dismissal, he walked over to check on his cows. "*No* isn't a word I have any problem understanding. As long as you actually say it, I'll understand it.''

Most of her nerves smoothed out. "All right, then, we—"

"But you'd better keep your guard up, Rebecca." He shot her a look that had all the nerves doubling back and sizzling. "Because I don't have any problem understanding a challenge, either. You want to play ghost hunter in my house, you take your chances. Willing to risk it?"

"You don't worry me."

His smile spread, slowly this time. "Yeah, I do. You're standing there right now wondering what in hell to do about me."

"Actually, I was wondering how you manage to walk around upright, when you're weighed down with that ego."

"Practice." Now he grinned. "Same way you manage it with all those heavy thoughts inside that head of yours. I'm just about finished up here. Why don't you go on in, make us some coffee? We can talk about this some more."

"I think we've covered it." She moved just quickly enough to get out ahead of him. "And I don't make coffee."

For a skinny woman, he mused, she looked mighty nice walking away. "Don't you want me to kiss you goodbye, sweetie?"

She tossed a look over her shoulder. "Kiss a cow, farm boy."

He couldn't resist. He was on her in a heartbeat, swinging her up into his arms and around in a dizzying circle while his laughter roared out. "You're the cutest damn thing."

Her breath had been lost somewhere during the first revolution. For an instant, all she could think was that his arms were as hard as rock, and felt absolutely wonderful. "I thought you understood *no*."

"I'm not kissing you, am I?" All innocence, Shane's eyes laughed into hers. "Unless you want me to. Just wanted to get a hold of you for a minute. I swear you weigh less than a sack of grain."

"Thank you so much for that poetic compliment. Put me down."

"You've really got to eat more. Why don't you hang around? I'll fix you some dinner."

"No," she said. "No, no, no."

"You only have to say it once." He cocked his head, enjoying the way the pulse in her throat beat like a bird's, just above the open collar of her silky white shirt. "Why are you trembling?"

"I'm angry."

"No, you're not." Intrigued now, he studied her face, and his voice gentled. "Did somebody hurt you?"

"No, of course not. I asked you to put me down."

"I'm going to. If I did what I wanted and carried you inside right now, I'd neglect my cows and break my word. I wouldn't want to do either." So he set her on her feet, but kept his hands on her shoulders. "It seems to me we've got something going here."

"I'd prefer to take my own time deciding that."

"That's fair." Because he was becoming fond of it, he skimmed a finger over her hair, tugged on one of the short, soft tresses. "It occurs to me that I've already decided. I really want you. Not being a psychiatrist or a heavy thinker, I don't have to analyze that or look for hidden meanings. I just feel it."

His eyes, green and dreamy, lowered to hers again, and held. "I want to take you to bed, and I want to make love with you. And I want it more every time I get near you. You can put that into your equation."

"I will." It was a struggle to concentrate when his hands were moving in gentle circles on her shoulders. "But it's not the only factor. Things would be . . . a lot less convoluted if we could back off from this while I'm getting my project under way."

"Less convoluted," he agreed, amused by the word. "And less fun."

Fun, she thought, feeling herself yearn toward him. It was a novel and interesting concept, when attached to intimacy.

He watched her lips curve just a little, felt her body soften, saw her eyes deepen. A knot of need twisted in him as he drew her closer. "Pretty Rebecca," he murmured, "let me show you—"

He could have committed murder when a sharp blast of a horn shattered the moment.

She stiffened, stepped back, as both of them looked over at the dusty compact that pulled up in front of the house. Rebecca had a clear view of the sulky-mouthed brunette who poked her gorgeous head out of the window.

"Shane, honey, I told you I'd try to drop by."

He lifted a hand in a casual wave, even as he felt the temperature surrounding him drop to the subzero range. "Ah, that's Darla. She's a friend of mine."

"I bet." The chip was back on Rebecca's shoulder, and it was the size of a redwood. She cocked a brow and curved her lips mockingly. He didn't have to know the mockery was for herself. "Don't let me keep you from your... friend, Shane, honey. I'm sure you're a very busy boy.''

''Look, damn it—''

Darla called out again, her husky voice a little impatient. Shane saw, with unaccustomed panic, that she was getting out of the car. With anyone else, the meeting would have been easy, even amusing. With Rebecca, he had a feeling it would be deadly. She'd eat Darla for breakfast.

''Listen, I—''

''I don't have time to look, or to listen,'' Rebecca said, interrupting him, desperately afraid she'd make a fool of herself in front of the stunning woman picking her way over the lawn in thin high heels. ''I have work to do. You and Darla have a nice visit.''

She strode off, leaving Shane caught between the willing and the wanted.

Chapter Six

During her stay at the inn, Rebecca had established a pattern. She rose early enough to join the other guests for breakfast. It wasn't the food, as marvelous as Cassie's cooking was, that nudged her out of bed and downstairs. She wanted the opportunity to interview her companions under the guise of a breezy morning chat.

It was work for her to keep it casual, not to fall into the habits of analyst or scientist. She'd been rewarded over coffee and waffles that morning by a young couple who both claimed to have felt a presence in the bridal suite during the night.

Now, alone in her room late at night, the inn quiet around her, Rebecca read over the notes she'd hurriedly made that morning.

Subjects corroborate each other's experience. Sudden cold, a strong scent of roses, the sound of a female weeping. Three senses involved. Subjects excited by experience rather than frightened. Very clear and firm when reporting each phenomenon. Neither claimed a sighting, but female subject described a sense of deep sadness which occurred just after temperature fluctuation and lasted until the scent of roses had faded.

Interesting, Rebecca mused as she worked the notes into a more formal style, including names and dates. As for herself, she'd slept like a baby, if only for a few short hours. She rarely slept more than five hours in any case, and the night before she had made do with three, in hopes of recording an event of her own.

But her room had remained comfortable and quiet throughout the night.

After her notes were refined, and her journal entry for the day was complete, she switched over to the book she was toying with writing. *The Haunting of Antietam.*

She rather liked the title, though she could picture some of her more illustrious colleagues muttering over it at faculty teas and university functions. Let them mutter, she thought. She'd toed the line all her life. It was time she did a little boat rocking.

It would be a new challenge to write something that was descriptive, even emotional, rather than dry and factual. To bring to life her vision, her impressions of the small town, with its quiet hills, the shadow of the mountains in the distance, those wide, fertile fields.

She needed to spend some time on the battlefield, absorb its ambience. But for now she had plenty to say about the inn, and its original inhabitants.

She worked for an hour, then two, losing herself in the story of the Barlows—the tragic Abigail, the unbending Charles, the children who had lost their mother at a tender age. Thanks to Cassie, Rebecca had another character to add. A man Abigail had loved and sent away. Rebecca suspected the man might have been of some authority in Antietam during that time. The sheriff, perhaps. It was too lovely a coincidence to overlook, and she intended to research it thoroughly.

She was so deep in her work that it took her several minutes to notice the hum of her equipment. Startled by it, she jerked back, stared at the monitor of her sensor.

Was that a draft? she wondered, and sprang up, shuddering. The temperature gauge was acutely sensitive. Rebecca watched with amazement as the numbers dropped rapidly from a comfortable seventy-two. She was hugging her arms by the time it reached thirty, and she could see her own breath puff out quickly as her heart thudded.

Yet she felt nothing but the cold. Nothing. She heard nothing, smelled nothing.

The lady doesn't come in here.

That was what Emma had told her. But did the master? It had to be Charles. She'd read so much about him, the thought filled her with a jumble of anger, fear and anticipation.

Moving quickly, Rebecca checked her recorder, the cameras. The quiet blip on a machine registered her presence and for an instant, an instant almost too quick to notice—something other.

Then it was gone, over, and warmth poured back into the room.

Nearly wild with excitement, she snatched up her recorder. "Event commenced at 2:08 and fifteen seconds, a.m., with dramatic temperature drop of forty-two degrees Fahrenheit. Barely measurable energy fluctuation lasting only a fraction of a second, followed by immediate rise in temperature. Event ended at 2:09 and twenty seconds, a.m. Duration of sixty-five seconds."

She stood for a moment, the recorder in her hand, trying to will it all to start again. She knew it had been Charles, she felt it, and her pulse was still scrambling. Dispassionately she wondered what her blood pressure would register.

"Come on, come on, you bully, you coward! You son of a bitch! Come back!"

The sound of her own voice, the raw intensity in it, had her forcing herself to take several deep breaths. Losing objectivity, she warned herself. Any project was doomed without objectivity.

So she made herself sit, monitored the equipment for another thirty minutes. Precisely she added the event to her records before shutting the computer down.

Too restless to sleep, she left her room. In the hall, she stood quietly, waiting, hoping, but there was only the dark and the stillness. She moved downstairs, lingering as she tried to envision the murdered Confederate soldier, the shocked Abigail, the terrified servants, the murdering Barlow.

They were all less substantial than thoughts to her.

She tried every room—the parlor where some said you could smell wood smoke from a fire that wasn't burning, the library, which both Regan and Cassie avoided as much as possible, because they felt uncomfortable there. In the solarium there was nothing but leafy plants, cozy chairs, and the light of the moon through the glass.

She struggled against discouragement as she wandered into the kitchen. There had been a moment, she reminded herself. She'd experienced it. Patience was as important as an open and curious mind.

She was drawn to the window, and that open and curious mind drifted past the gardens and the lawn, through the trees, to the fields beyond. And the house where Shane was sleeping.

The urge was so strong it shocked her. The urge to go out, walk over that grass, over those fields. She wanted to go into that house, to go to him. Foolishness, she told herself. It was doubtful he was alone. She imagined he was snuggled up with that beautiful brunette, or some other equally appealing woman, for the night.

But still the urge was there, so powerful, so elementally physical it brought an ache to her belly. Was it the place that pulled at her? she wondered. Or the man?

It was something to think about. Something she would have to gather the courage to explore. No more mousy, fade-into-the-corner Rebecca, she thought. No more spending her life huddled behind a desk or a handy book. Experience was what she'd come here for. And if Shane MacKade offered experience, she'd sample it.

In her own time, of course. At her own pace.

He saw her as a woman who could hold her own with him, and she was going to find a way to do exactly that.

He wanted to take her to bed.

How does that make you feel, Dr. Knight?

Frightened, exhilarated, curious.

Frightened, you say. Of the sexual experience?

Sex is a basic biological function, a human experience. Why would I be frightened of it? Because it remains unknown, she answered herself. So it frightens, exhilarates and stirs the curiosity. He stirs the curiosity. Once I have control of the situation—

Ah, Dr. Knight, so it's a matter of control? How do you feel about the possible loss of control?

Uncomfortable, which is why I don't intend to lose it.

She blew out a breath, shut off the questioning part of her brain. But she couldn't quite shut off that nagging urge, so she walked quickly out of the kitchen and went upstairs to bed.

But she dreamed, and the dreams were full of laughter....

A man's arms around her, the two of them rolling over a soft, giving mattress like wrestling children. Giggles muffled against warm lips, teasing fingers combing through her long, tangled hair.

Hush, John, you'll wake the baby.

You're making all the noise.

Quick hands sneaking under her cotton nightgown, finding wonderful spots to linger.

You've got too many clothes on, Sarah. I want you naked.

Mock slaps and tussles, more giggles.

I'm still carrying around extra weight from the baby.

You're perfect. He's perfect. God, I want you. I want you, Sarah. I love you. Let me love you.

While the laughter stilled, the joy didn't. And the soft feather bed gave quietly beneath the weight and rhythm of mating....

She was groggy the next day, not from lack of sleep, but from the dream that wouldn't quite leave her. For most of the afternoon she closeted herself in her room, using her modem to call up snatches of data on the population of Antietam, circa 1862.

Her printer was happily spewing out a list of names from census, birth and death registries when Cassie knocked on the door.

"I'm sorry to bother you."

"No, that's fine." Distracted, Rebecca peered through her glasses. "I'm trying to find Abigail's lover—if she had one."

"Oh." Obviously flustered, Cassie ran a hand through her hair. "But how would you be able to?"

"Process of elimination—ages, marital status." Remembering, she took the glasses off, and Cassie popped into focus. "You seemed awfully sure he didn't have a wife."

"No, he couldn't have."

"And he wasn't in the army, but you said something about him resigning some kind of post when he left town."

"It's so odd to hear you talk about it, about them, as if they were real and here."

Rebecca smiled and leaned back in her chair. "Aren't they?"

"Well, yes, I suppose they are." Cassie shook her head. "I get caught up in the story. I came to tell you I have to run to the hospital."

"Hospital?" Alarmed, Rebecca shot out of her chair. "Is one of the children hurt? Sick?"

"Oh, no, no. Shane—"

"He's had an accident." Rebecca's face went dead white. "Where is he? What happened?"

"Rebecca, it's Savannah. She's in labor." Curious, Cassie watched Rebecca sink bonelessly back into her chair. "I didn't mean to frighten you."

"It's all right." Weakly she waved a hand. "I'm supposed to know better than to jump to conclusions."

"Shane called a couple of hours ago after Jared called him. I needed to arrange for a sitter before I could go. I'm going to drop Connor and Emma off with Ed at the diner. You haven't met Ed yet. She's just wonderful. She can't handle Ally, too, but there's day care at the hospital."

"Uh-huh." Rebecca had nearly recovered.

"I didn't want you to think you'd been deserted. There's some cold cuts and a pie in the kitchen, if you get hungry. I have to take the car, but I'm supposed to tell you that you can go over to the cabin, or the farm, and borrow one if you need to go out."

"I don't need to go anywhere." Calm again, she smiled. "Savannah's having her baby. That's wonderful. Is everything all right?"

"Fine, at last report. It's just that we all want to be there."

"Of course you do. Give mother and father my best. I'd be happy to keep Ally for you, if you like."

"That's awfully nice of you. But I'm nursing, and I don't know how long I'll be." Cassie nibbled her bottom lip as she began to organize things in her head. "We're not expecting any new guests, and I've left a note for the ones who are out and about today. I usually serve tea in about an hour, but..."

"Don't worry, we'll fend for ourselves. Go on, Cassie, I can see you're dying to be there."

"There's nothing like a new baby."

"No, I'm sure there isn't."

When she was alone, Rebecca tried to concentrate, but she could visualize it all. The whole MacKade family would be pacing the waiting room, probably driving the nursing staff to distraction. They'd be noisy, of course. One of them would pop into the birthing room to check the progress, and come out and report to the others.

All of them would enjoy every minute of it. That was what close families did, enjoy each other. She wondered if they had any idea how lucky they were.

She put in another two hours at the computer, easily eliminated half the male names on her list before hunger had her wandering down to the kitchen.

Some of the other guests had already sampled the pie Cassie had left. And someone had been considerate enough to leave coffee on. She poured a cup, thought about building a sandwich, and settled for blueberries baked in a flaky crust.

When the phone rang, she answered automatically. "Hello. Oh, MacKade Inn."

"You've got a good, sexy voice for the phone, Rebecca."

"Shane?"

"And a good ear. We thought you'd want to know the MacKades just increased by one."

"What did she have? How is she?"

"A girl, and they're both terrific. Miranda Mac-Kade is eight pounds, two ounces and twenty-one inches of gorgeous female."

"Miranda." Rebecca sighed. "That's lovely."

"Cassie's on her way back, but she might be a while yet, picking up the kids, telling Ed all the details and all. I thought you might be wondering."

"I was. Thanks."

"I'm in the mood to celebrate. Want to celebrate with me, Dr. Knight?"

"Ah . . ."

"Nothing fancy, I didn't have time to change before. I can swing by, pick you up. Buy you a beer."

"That's sounds irresistible, but—"

"Good. Half an hour."

"I didn't say—" She could only frown at the rude buzz of the dial tone.

She wouldn't primp. Sheer vanity had her doing a quick check in the mirror and giving her makeup a buff, but that was all he was getting. The leggings and thin fawn-colored sweater she'd worked in that evening were comfortable, and would certainly do for a casual beer.

If she dressed them up with big copper-and-brass earrings, it was for her own benefit. She'd begun to enjoy the ritual of decorating her body over the past few months.

She left a note for Cassie on her door, then walked out of the inn to wait for Shane.

Hints of the coming fall brought a tang on the air. The day had been hot and still, but now the air was cool. The darkness was soft and complete, as it was meant to be in the country.

Occasionally a car would rumble by on the road below the steep lane. Then silence would fall again, beautifully.

She'd been sure she would miss the noise of the city, the comforting grumble of life, the periodic and cheerful rudeness of it. In New York, she'd finally taught herself to join in that life, to spend time in the stores and museums, to brush up against people instead of shying away from them. It was a kind of therapy she'd prescribed for herself, and it had worked.

She'd stopped walking with her eyes on her own feet, stopped hurrying back to her own apartment, where she could be safe and alone with her books.

But she didn't miss it. She liked the quiet here, the slower pace, and the opportunity to get to know people. Now she was going to have a drink with a very attractive man.

All in all, it wasn't a bad end to a productive day.

She watched the headlights come and veer toward the lane. Shifting her shoulder bag, she headed toward the truck.

"That's what I like to see, a woman waiting for me."

"Sorry to disappoint you." She hiked herself up and into the cab of the truck. "I wanted to enjoy the incredible weather. It's starting to smell like fall."

"You look pretty." Reaching over, he flicked a finger over her earring and sent it dancing.

"So do you." It was absolutely true—the stubby ponytail, the faded work shirt, the easy grin. "Where are we going?"

"Just down to Duff's." Shane slung an arm over the back of the seat and set the truck in reverse. "It's not much, but it's home."

It certainly wasn't much, Rebecca decided at first study. The tavern was badly lit, with glaring fluorescent lights over the pool table that were only softened by the clouds of smoke from cigarettes. A jukebox that blared out whiny country music. The decorations ran to scattered peanut shells, posters for beer, and an oddly charming print of dogs playing poker. The air smelled stale, and a little dangerous.

She liked it.

On their way to the bar, a scarred affair guarded by a scrawny man with an irritable look on his face, Shane introduced her to half a dozen people.

She got the look outsiders are greeted by in a close-knit community—a combination of curiosity, distrust and interest. Someone called out for Shane to pick up a cue, but he shook his head and held up two fingers to the man behind the bar.

"How's it going, Duff?"

The skinny bartender grunted as he popped the tops of two bottles. "Usual."

"This is Rebecca, a friend of Regan's from New York."

"New York City's a hellhole."

"You've been there?" Rebecca asked politely.

"Couldn't pay me to set foot in it." He slid the bottles over the bar and went back to scowling at his customers.

"Duff's a real chatterbox," Shane commented as he led the way to a table. "And the happiest man in town."

"I could tell right off." She took her seat. "After all, I'm a professional."

Grinning, Shane tapped his bottle to hers. "To Miranda Catherine MacKade."

In concert, Rebecca lifted the bottle and sipped. "So, tell me all about it."

"Well, the couple of times I got in to see her, Savannah was a little cranky. She said MacKade men should be locked up—among other things that had to do with specific parts of the anatomy."

"Sounds fair, coming from a woman in labor."

"Yeah, well, Regan and Cassie weren't quite so nasty. Then again, Savannah's a little more out there. Anyway, she spit nails for a while. Then, after it was over, she was cooing rose petals."

"And Jared?"

"Went from sweating bullets to grinning like a demented fool. That's the way it goes every time we have a baby."

"We?"

"It's a family affair. You could have come."

"It sounds like Savannah had enough company." She tilted her head. "So, does it give you any ideas?"

"Huh? Oh." He leaned back, grinning. "It gives me the idea that my brothers are doing a fine job making families. No need for me to horn in. What about you? You thinking about settling down and hatching a brood?"

"Hatching a brood?" She had to laugh. "No."

Shane took a peanut from the plastic bowl on the table, cracked it. "So, what do you do when you're not shrinking heads or chasing ghosts or giving lectures?''

"I live in a hellhole, remember? There's always plenty to do. Muggings, murders, orgies. My life's very full.''

He skimmed a hand over hers. "Anyone in particular helping fill it out?''

"No. No one in particular." She smiled sweetly, leaned forward. "How's Darla?''

He cleared his throat and bought himself a little time by sipping his beer. "She's fine. Dandy.''

It wasn't worth mentioning that he'd nudged good old Darla along, despite her invitation to fix his supper—and anything else he might like. "Any progress on the hunt?''

"That's not a very subtle avoidance of the topic.''

"I wasn't trying to be subtle." He laid his hand over hers again, snagging her fingers before she could draw them away. "Find any good ghosts lately?''

"Actually, I did." She had the pleasure of seeing the smile fade from his eyes.

"That's bull.''

"No, indeed. I have some very nice documentation of an event. Registered a forty-two-degree temperature drop in less than two minutes.''

He took another drink. "Your fancy equipment needs to be overhauled.''

His reaction amused her, intrigued her. "You're very resistant. Do you feel threatened?''

"Why would I feel threatened by something that doesn't exist?''

One brow cocked up under her fringe of bangs. "Why would you?''

"Because I—" He caught himself, narrowed his eyes. She was smiling blandly and, he noted, very much in control. "Is that how you analyze your patients?"

"Do you feel like a patient?"

"Cut it out."

"Sorry." She threw her head back and laughed. "It was irresistible. I don't really do individual therapy, but you'd make a terrific subject. Want to try word-association?"

"No."

She arched both brows this time. "You're not afraid, are you? It's very simple. I say a word, you respond with the first thing that comes to mind."

"I'm not afraid of some silly parlor game." But he was irritated, just enough to jerk his shoulders. "Fine. Shoot."

"Home."

"Family."

It made her smile. "Bird."

"Feather."

"Car."

"Truck."

"City."

"Noise."

"Country."

"Land."

"Sex."

"Women." Then he brought their joined hands to his lips, nipped lightly at her fingers. "Rebecca."

She ignored the jingling spurt of her pulse. "It's the first thing that comes to your mind that counts. All in all, I'd say you're a very elemental man, set in your ways and happy with them. Consider that a thumb-nail analysis."

"Why don't I try it with you?"

"As soon as you get your degree, farm boy." She waited a beat. "If you're hungry, why don't you try the peanuts?"

"I like your hand better." To prove it, he continued to nibble, all the way around to her palm. "It's long and a little bony. Like the rest of you."

In a casual move, she scooted her chair closer, leaned her head toward his. "Do you really think I'd let you seduce me over a couple of beers at the local tavern?"

"It's worth a shot." He brushed his lips over her wrist. "Your pulse is racing, Dr. Knight."

"A basic chemical reaction to stimulus. Nothing personal."

"We could make it personal." He glanced over his shoulder, saw that the pool table was free. "You up for a bet?"

"Depends on the type of bet."

"How about a game of pool, a friendly wager?"

"Pool?" Her brows drew together. "I don't know the rules."

Even better, he thought. "I'll explain them. You're supposed to be a quick study. Anybody smart enough to have a bunch of initials after their name should be able to learn a simple game."

"All right. What's the bet?"

"I win, we go out to my truck and neck. I'm really hankering for a taste of you."

She took a slow breath, made sure her eyes stayed cool. "And if I win?"

"What's your pleasure?"

She considered, then smiled. "When I move my equipment over to the farm, you'll help me with my project, on a purely professional level."

"Sure." With the confidence of a veteran hustler, he rose and led her over to the table. "Since you're a beginner, I'll spot you two balls."

"That's generous," she said, without having a clue whether it was or not.

Being a fair man, and one who rarely lost at this particular game, he explained the procedure carefully. That also gave him the opportunity to snuggle up behind her, his mouth at her ear as he gave her instructions on how to hold and use the cue.

"You want control," he told her, sniffing her hair. "But you don't want to force it. Keep the stroke smooth."

She tried to ignore the fact that her bottom was snug against him and, following his guiding hands, struck the cue ball.

"Nice," he murmured. "You've got good form. And great ears." He nipped at one before she straightened. But when she turned, rather than backing away, he set his hands comfortably on her hips. "Why don't we pretend we played and just go neck?"

"A bet's a bet. Back off, farm boy."

"I can wait," he said cheerfully. He could already imagine wrapping himself around her and steaming up the windows in the truck. "You want to break?"

"I'll leave that to you." She stepped away, chalked her cue as he did.

The rules were simple enough, she mused. You were either solid or striped, depending on which type of ball you managed to sink first. Then you just kept sinking them, avoiding the black eight ball. If you hit that in before the rest were dispatched—unless you struck it with another ball first—you lost.

Otherwise, whoever sank all their balls first, then the eight, won.

She watched Shane lean over the table, long legs, long arms, big hands. The look of him distracted her enough that she didn't see how he broke the triangle of balls, but she did see the results. Three balls thumped into pockets, and he called solids.

Lips pursed, she studied his technique, the speed and direction of balls rolling over the green felt. She'd seen the game played, of course. There was a billiard table in the country club where her parents had a membership. But she'd never paid much attention.

It was obviously simple geometry and applied physics, she decided. Quick calculations, a steady hand and a good eye were all that was required.

Shane pocketed another two balls before he glanced at her. Her brow was furrowed, her head cocked. It was interesting to watch her think, he mused. It would be even more interesting to watch her feel. But it wasn't quite fair to run the table on her when she hadn't even had a chance to shoot.

To balance the scales a bit, he attempted a nearly impossible shot. He nearly made it, but his ball kissed the corner of the pocket and rolled clear.

"You're up, Doc."

He moved around the table to help her with her stance, but she shrugged him away. "I'd rather do it myself."

"Fine." He smiled at her with affection, and superiority. "You should go for the one with the yellow stripe. It's a clean shot into the side pocket."

"I see it." Muttering to herself, she leaned over the table, took careful aim, squinting a bit to keep the balls in focus, and sent it in.

"Nice." Genuinely pleased, he walked back to their table to fetch the beer. "You even left your cue ball in good position for the next shot. If you—"

She lifted her head, aimed a bland look in his direction. "Do you mind?"

"Hey." He lifted a hand, palm out. "Just trying to help. You go on ahead."

He did cluck his tongue a bit as she set up for a bank shot. Couldn't the woman see her three ball was clear? He lifted his beer to hide his grin. At this rate, he was going to have her exactly where he wanted in five minutes.

Then his mouth dropped open. She banked the ball against the side and sent it at a clean angle into the corner pocket. She didn't so much as smile, never glanced up, but went directly back to work.

A few customers roused themselves to wander over to watch, and to kibitz. They might have been as invisible as her ghosts.

She played systematically, pausing only briefly between shots, with her brows knit and her eyes unfocused, as she circled the table. He forgot the beer that was dangling from his fingers, suffered the elbow nudges and comments from onlookers as she quickly, quietly, and without a hitch, cleaned house.

To add insult to injury, she used one of his own balls, the one he could—and should—have sent home when he was feeling sorry for her, to knock the eight ball into the pocket and trounce him at his own game.

Lips pursed, she straightened, scanned the table. "Is that it?"

There were hoots of laugher. Several men patted her shoulder and offered to buy her a beer. Shane merely propped his cue on the table.

"Is this how you worked your way through college? Hustling pool?"

Flushed with success now that the work was done, she beamed at him. "No, I had numerous scholarships, and a generous college fund. I've never played pool before in my life."

"I'll be damned." He dipped his hands in his pockets, studying her. "You ran the table. That wasn't luck, beginner's or otherwise."

"No, it wasn't. It was science. The game is based on angles and velocity, isn't it?" Delighted with the fresh knowledge, she ran a hand through her hair. "Want to play again? I could spot you two balls this time."

He started to swear, but couldn't resist the laugh. "What the hell! We'll go for two out of three."

Chapter Seven

"So we played pool." Rebecca was busily adjusting one of her cameras in Shane's kitchen while Regan looked on. "He's really very good. We ended up closing the place down."

Regan waited a moment, tugged her ear as if to clear it. "You played pool—at Duff's."

"Uh-huh. We were just going to play one game, then it was two out of three, and three out of five, and so forth. It's great fun. But I couldn't let all those men buy me beers. I'd have been flat on my face."

"Men were buying you beer."

"Well, they wanted to, but I'm not much of a drinker." Lips pursed, Rebecca stepped back to check the positioning. "Shane was awfully good-natured about it all. A lot of people get annoyed when you beat them at their own game."

"Excuse me." Regan held up a hand. "You *beat* Shane—that's Shane MacKade—at pool."

"Seven out of ten—I think. Do you know how to work this coffee maker?"

Leave the woman alone for a few days and look what she gets into, Regan thought. "She can't make coffee, but she can beat Shane at pool. The only person I've ever known to beat Shane is Rafe—and nobody beats Rafe."

"Bet I could." Smug, Rebecca flashed a grin. "I'm a natural. Charlie Dodd said so."

"Charlie Dodd?" Measuring out coffee, Regan laughed. "You hung out with Charlie Dodd and the boys at Duff's, playing pool? What in the world were you doing there?"

"Celebrating Miranda's birth. Anyway, since I won the bet, Shane has to help me with my project. He's not terribly happy about it. He has a definite block about anything supernatural."

Curiouser and curiouser, Regan mused. "One minor detail."

"Hmm?"

"What if you'd lost the bet?"

"I'd have necked with him in his truck."

Regan splashed the water she'd been pouring into the coffee maker all over the counter. "Good Lord, Rebecca, what has happened to you?"

A smile ghosting around her mouth, Rebecca looked dreamily out the window. "I might have enjoyed it."

"I've no doubt you would have." After blowing out a breath, Regan mopped up the spill and started again. "Honey, I don't want to interfere in your life, but Shane... He's very smooth with women—and he doesn't tend to take relationships seriously.''

Rebecca caught herself dreaming, and stopped. ''I know. Don't worry about me. I've been sheltered and secluded, but I'm not stupid.'' She leaned over to coo at the baby napping in his carrier. ''I think I'm handling Shane very well, all in all. I may have an affair with him.''

''You may have an affair with him,'' Regan repeated slowly. ''Am I having some sort of out-of-body experience?''

''I hope you'll give me all the details, if you are.''

Regan rubbed a hand over her face, told herself to be rational. But it was Rebecca, she thought, who was always rational. ''You may have an affair, with Shane. That's Shane MacKade. My brother-in-law.''

''Um-hmm...'' Unable to resist, Rebecca skimmed a fingertip over Jason's soft, round cheek. ''I'm still considering it. But he's very attractive, and, I'm sure, very skilled.'' The fingertip wasn't enough, so she bent to touch her lips lightly to the same lovely spot. ''If I'm going to have an affair, it should be with someone I like, respect and have some affection for, don't you agree?''

''Well, yes, in the general scheme of things, but...''

Rebecca straightened and grinned. ''And if he's gorgeous and clever in bed, so much the better. A terrific face and body aren't everything, of course, but they are a nice bonus. I'd theorize that the stronger the physical attraction, the better the sex.''

The coffeepot was gurgling away before Regan found the words. ''Rebecca, making love with a man isn't an experiment, or a science project.''

THE $1,000,000.00 PLUS JACKPOT!

IT'S FUN! BIG BUCK$

IT'S FREE!

HOW TO PLAY

It's so easy...grab a Lucky coin, and go right to your BIG BUCKS game card. Scratch off silver squares in a STRAIGHT LINE (across, down, or diagonal) until 5 dollar signs are revealed. BINGO...Doing this makes you eligible for a chance to win $1,000,000.00 in lifetime-income ($33,333.33 each year for 30 years!) Also scratch all 4 corners to reveal the dollar signs. This entitles you to a chance to win the $50,000.00 Extra Bonus Prize! Void if more than 9 squares scratched off.

Return your game card and we'll assign you a unique Sweepstakes Number, so it's important that your name and address section is completed correctly. This will permit us to identify you and match you with any cash prize rightfully yours! (SEE BACK OF BOOK FOR DETAILS.)

FREE BOOKS PLUS FREE GIFTS!

At the same time you play your BIG BUCKS game card for BIG CASH PRIZES...scratch the Lucky Charm to receive FOUR FREE

Silhouette Special Edition® novels, and a FREE GIFT, TOO! They're totally free, absolutely free with no obligation to buy anything!

These books have a cover price of $4.50 each. But THEY ARE TOTALLY FREE; even the shipping will be at our expense! The Silhouette Reader Service™ is not like some book clubs. You don't have to buy any minimum number of purchases–not even one!

The fact is, thousands of readers look forward to receiving six of the best new romance novels each month and they love our discount prices!

Of course you may play BIG BUCKS for cash prizes alone by not scratching off your Lucky Charm, but why not get everything that we are offering and that you are entitled to! You'll be glad you did.

Offer limited to one per household and not valid to current Silhouette Special Edition® subscribers. All orders subject to approval.

BIG BUCKS

S

▶ DETACH AND MAIL CARD TODAY!

HURRY!
This jackpot must be claimed!

Scratch here →

YES! I have played my BIG BUCKS game card as instructed. Enter me in the MILLION DOLLAR Sweepstakes and also enter me for the Extra Bonus Prize. When winners are selected, tell me if I've won. If the Lucky Charm is scratched off I will also receive everything revealed, as explained on the back of this page.

LUCKY CHARM GAME!

Claim
4 FREE Books
AND a FREE
Mystery Gift!

335 CIS AYZ3
(C-SIL-SE-04/96)

NAME _____

ADDRESS _____ APT. _____

CITY _____ PROV. _____ POSTAL CODE _____

TWO WAYS TO WIN BIG BUCKS!

1. Uncover 5 $ signs in a row . . . BINGO! You're eligible for a chance to win the $1,000,000.00 SWEEPSTAKES!

2. Uncover 5 $ signs in a row AND uncover $ signs in all 4 corners . . . BINGO! You're also eligible for a chance to win the $50,000.00 EXTRA BONUS PRIZE!

THE SILHOUETTE READER SERVICE™: HERE'S HOW IT WORKS

Accepting free books places you under no obligation to buy anything. You may keep the books and gift and return the shipping statement marked "cancel". If you do not cancel, about a month later we will send you 6 additional novels and bill you just $3.46 each plus 25¢ delivery and GST*. That's the complete price, and – compared to cover prices of $4.50 each – quite a bargain! You may cancel at any time, but if you choose to continue, every month we'll send you 6 more books, which you may either purchase at the discount price...or return at our expense and cancel your subscription.

*Terms and prices subject to change without notice. Canadian residents add applicable provincial taxes and GST.

"In a way it is." Then she laughed and crossed over to take Regan by the shoulders. There seemed to be no way to explain, even to Regan, what it was like to feel this way. Free and able and attractive. "Stop worrying about me, Mama. I'm all grown up now."

"Yes, obviously."

"I want to explore possibilities, Regan. I've done what I was told, what was expected of me, for so long. Forever. I need to do what I want." With a little sigh, she took a turn around the kitchen. "That's what this is all about. Why do you think I chose the paranormal as a hobby? A first-year psych student could figure it out. All of my life has been so abnormal, and at the same time so tediously normal. *I* was abnormal."

"That's not true." Regan's voice was sharp and annoyed, and made Rebecca smile.

"You always did stand up for me, even against myself. But it is true. It's not normal for a seven-year-old to do calculus, Regan, or to be able to discuss the political ramifications of the Crimean War with historians, in French. I'm not even sure what normal behavior is for a seven-year-old, except in theory, because I never was one."

Before Regan could speak, she shook her head and hurried on. "I was pushed into everything so young. You can't know what it's like to go to school year-round, year after year. Even when I was at home, there were tutors and projects, assignments, and before I knew it my whole life was study, work, lecture." She lifted her hands, let them fall. "Earn a degree, earn another, then go home alone."

"I didn't know you were so unhappy," Regan murmured.

"I've been miserable all my life." Rebecca closed her eyes. "Oh, that sounds so pathetic. It's not fair, I suppose. I've had tremendous advantages. Education, money, respect, opportunities. But advantages can trap you, Regan. Just as disadvantages can. It seems petty to complain about them, but I am. Now I'm doing something about it, finally." With a kind of triumph, she drew in a deep, greedy breath. "I'm doing something no one expects from me, something to give my stuffy, straight-arrow colleagues a marvelous chance to gossip. And something that fascinates me."

"I'm all for it." But Regan was worried as she opened cupboards for mugs. "I think it's wonderful that you've taken time for yourself, that you have an interest in something most people consider out of the ordinary."

Rebecca accepted the mug of coffee. "But?"

"But Shane doesn't come under the heading of Hobby. He's the sweetest man I know, but he could hurt you."

Rebecca mulled it over as she sipped. "It's a possibility. But even that would be an experience. I've never been close enough to a man to be hurt by one."

She moved over to the window to look out. She could see him, in the field, riding a tractor. Just as she'd imagined. No, it wasn't a tractor, she remembered. A baler. He'd be making hay.

"I love looking at him," she murmured.

"None of them are hard on the eyes," Regan commented as she joined Rebecca at the window. "And none of them are easy on the heart." She laid a hand on Rebecca's shoulder. "Just be careful."

But Rebecca felt she'd been careful too long already.

She couldn't even cook. Shane had never known anyone who was incapable of doing more at a stove than heating up a can of soup. And even that, for Rebecca, was a project of momentous proportions.

He didn't mind her being there. He'd talked himself into that. He liked her company, was certain he would eventually charm her into bed, but he hated her reasons for moving in.

Her equipment was everywhere—in the kitchen, the living room, in the guest room. He couldn't walk through his own house without facing a camera.

It baffled him that an obviously intelligent woman actually believed she was going to take videos of ghosts.

Still, there were some advantages. If he cooked, she cheerfully did the clearing-up. And it wasn't a hardship to come in from the fields or the barn and find her at the kitchen table, making her notes on her little laptop computer.

She claimed she felt most at home in the kitchen— though she didn't know a skillet from a saucepan—so she spent most of her time there.

He'd gotten through the first night, though it was true that he'd done a great deal of tossing and turning at the idea that she was just down the hall. And if he'd been gritty-eyed and cranky the next morning, he'd worked it off by the time he finished the milking and came in to cook breakfast.

And she came down for breakfast, he reflected. Though she didn't eat much—barely, in his opinion, enough to sustain life. But she drank coffee, shared the morning paper with him, asked questions. Lord, the woman was full of questions.

Still, it was pleasant to have company over the first meal of the day. Someone who looked good, smelled good, had something to say for herself. The problem was, he found himself thinking about how she had looked, had smelled, what she had said, when he went out to work.

He couldn't remember another woman hanging in his mind quite so long, or quite so strongly. That was something that could worry a man, if he let it.

Shane MacKade didn't like to worry. And he wasn't used to thinking about a woman who didn't seem to be giving him the same amount of attention.

It was simply a matter of adjustment—or so he told himself. She was a guest in his home now, and a man didn't take advantage of a guest. Which was why he wanted her out again as soon as possible—so that he could.

And if he just didn't think overmuch about how pretty she looked, tapping away at her keyboard, those little round glasses perched on her nose, the eyes behind them dark with concentration, her long, narrow feet crossed neatly at the ankles, he didn't suffer.

But, damn it, how was he supposed to *not* think about it?

When he banged a pot for the third time, Rebecca tipped down her glasses and peered at him over them. "Shane, I don't want you to feel that you have to cook for me."

"You're not going to do it," he muttered.

"I can dial the telephone. Why don't I order something and have it delivered?"

He turned then, his eyes bland. "You're not in New York now, sweetie. Nobody delivers out here."

"Oh." She let out a little sigh, took off her glasses. There was tension radiating from him. Then again, there was always something radiating from him. He was the most . . . alive, she decided . . . man she'd ever come across.

And right now he seemed terribly tense. Probably a cow problem. Sympathetic, she rose to go over and rub his shoulders. "You've had a rough one. It must be tiring working in the fields like that, hours on end, then dealing with the stock."

"It's easier on a decent night's sleep," he said through gritted teeth. Her bony hands were only tensing muscles that already ached.

"You're awfully tight. Why don't you sit down? I'll open a can of something, make sandwiches."

"I don't want a sandwich."

"It's the best I can do."

He spun around, caught her. "I want you."

Her heart lurched, did a quick, nervous jig in her throat before she managed to swallow it. "Yes, I believe we've established that." She didn't gulp audibly, didn't tremble noticeably. The temper in his eyes was easier to face than the passion beneath it. "You also agreed to a professional atmosphere."

"I know what I agreed to." His eyes, green and stormy, bored into hers. "I don't have to like it."

"No, you don't. Has it occurred to you that you're angry because I'm not reacting in the manner you're accustomed to having women react?"

"We're not talking about women. We're talking about you. You and me, here and now."

"We're talking about sex," she answered, and gave his arms a squeeze before backing away. "And I'm considering it."

"Considering it?" He could have throttled her. "What, like considering whether to have chicken or fish for dinner? Nobody's that cold-blooded."

"It's sensible. Deal with it." With a jerk of her shoulder, she went back to the table and sat.

Deal with it? he thought, boiling over. "Is that right? So you'll let me know when you've finished considering and come to a conclusion?"

"You'll be the first," she told him, and slipped on her glasses.

He battled back temper. It was a hard war to win, for a MacKade. Cold-blooded reason was what she understood, he decided. So he'd give it to her, and hoped she choked on it.

"You know, now that I'm considering, it occurs to me that you may be a little cool for my taste, and definitely bony. I like a warmer, softer sort."

She felt her jaw clench, then deliberately relaxed it. "A good try, farm boy. Uninterest, insult and challenge. I'm sure it works a good percentage of the time." She made herself smile at him. "But you're going to have to do better with me."

"Right now, I'll do better without you." Since he obviously wasn't going to win where he was, he strode to the door and out. All he needed was to decide which one of his brothers to go pick a fight with.

Rebecca let out a long breath and took her glasses off so that she could rub her hands over her face. That, she thought, had been a close one. How could she have known that the barely controlled fury, the frazzled desire, that absolutely innate arrogance of his, would be so exciting, so endearing?

She'd almost given in. The instant he whirled around and grabbed her, she might have thrown any lingering doubts to the winds. But...

There would have been no way to control any part of the situation, with him in that volatile mood. She would have been taken. And as glorious as that sounded in theory, she was afraid of the fact.

If he only knew she was waiting now only to settle her own nerves and to be certain he was calm. She knew that when Shane was calm, and amused, he would be a delightful and tender lover. Edgy and needy, he'd be demanding, impatient.

So they would both wait until the moment was right.

She sat back, her eyes closed. It was peaceful now, with that whirlwind Shane could create around him gone. She missed it, a little, even as she reveled in the quiet. She found it so easy to relax here, in this room, in this house. Even the creak of the boards settling at night was comforting.

And the smell of wood smoke and meat cooking, the hint of cinnamon and apple, the muffled crackle of the fire behind the door of the stove. Such things made home home, after all....

She froze, her eyes still closed, her body as tense as a stretched wire. Nothing was cooking, so why could she smell it? There was no fire, so why could she hear it?

Slowly she opened her eyes. For a moment, the room seemed to waver and her vision dimmed. A cast-iron stove, a fire in the raised hearth. Pies cooling on the wide windowsill, and the sun streaming in.

A blink, and it was gone. Tile and wood, the hum of the refrigerator.

Yet the scents remained, clear, strong. Like an echo deep in her mind, she thought she heard a baby's fretful crying.

"All right, Rebecca," she said shakily. "You wanted it. Looks like you've got it."

Rising quickly, she darted into the living room. Amid the cozy chairs, the rocker, the books stacked haphazardly on shelves, was equipment. There'd been no temperature drop registered, but energy was crackling. She didn't need a gauge to tell her, she could feel it. Electricity singing along her skin, bringing the hair on the nape of her neck stiffly up.

She wasn't alone.

The baby was crying. With a hand pressed to her mouth, she stared at her recorder. Would she hear that piping wail on tape when she played it back? Upstairs, one of the bedroom doors closed quietly. She could hear the squeak and roll of a rocker over wood, and the crying died.

The baby's being rocked, she thought, almost giddy with delight. Soothed, loved. That was what she felt through all the energy, all the excitement. Love, deep, abiding and rich. The house was alive with it.

Tears trailed down her cheeks as the warmth of it enfolded her.

When it was quiet again, when she was alone again, she picked up the recorder and reported. Back at her laptop, she detailed every instant of the event and copied it to disk.

Then she got a bottle of wine from the refrigerator and celebrated her success.

* * *

It was nearly midnight when Shane got back, and she was right where he'd left her. He'd vented most of his temper. No one had been much interested in a fight, but Devin had managed to joke him out of his foul mood.

He was afraid it might come back now that he was faced with her, sitting there smiling, her hair tousled from her hands, her glasses slipping down her nose.

"Don't you ever quit?"

"I'm obsessive-compulsive," she said, very carefully. "Hi."

"Hi." His brows drew together as he noted the flushed cheeks and sloppy grin. "What are you doing?"

"Nothing. I've been playing with the ghosts. They're very friendly ghosts, much nicer than the Barlows."

He came closer. There was a bottle of wine next to her computer, all but empty. And a glass half-full. He took another, closer look at her face and snorted out a laugh.

"You're plowed, Dr. Knight."

"Does that mean drunk? If so, I'm forced to agree with your diagnosis. I'm very, very, *very* drunk." She lifted the glass, managed to sip without pouring it down the front of her shirt. "I don't know how it happened. Prob'ly 'cause I kept drinking."

Lord, she was cute, sprawled in the chair, her eyes all bright and glowing. Her smile was...well, he thought, stupid. It was satisfying to realize that she could be stupid about something.

"That'll do it." Gently he braced a finger under her chin to keep her head from wobbling. "Did you eat anything?"

"Nope. Can't cook." That was so funny she sputtered with laughter. "Hi."

"Yeah, hi." It was impossible to be angry with her now. She looked so sweet, and so incredibly drunk. He slipped the glasses the rest of the way off her nose and set them aside. "Let's get you upstairs, baby."

"Aren't you going to kiss me?" With that, she slid gracefully from chair to floor.

With a good-natured oath, he reached down to pick her up. She might be drunk, but she had damn good aim. Her mouth fastened on his in a long, sucking, eye-popping kiss.

"Mmm... You're so...tasty." Riding on that taste, and on the wine swimming in her head, she flung out her arms to fasten them around his neck. "Come down here, okay? And kiss me again. It just makes my head go all funny, and my heart pound. Want to feel my heart pound?" She snatched his hand and slapped it over her breast. "Feel that?"

Yeah, he could feel it all right. "Cut it out." His system was jangled, and he had to hold on to honor with a slippery fist. "You're impaired, sweetie."

"I feel wonderful. Don't you want to feel me?"

This time his curse wasn't quite as good-natured. He hauled her up, and couldn't avoid the cheerful kisses she plastered over his face and neck.

"Stop it, Rebecca." His voice cracked with desperation as his body went on red alert. "Behave yourself."

"Don't want to. Always behaving. Tired of it. Let me just get this off for you." With more enthusiasm than finesse, she fumbled at the buttons of his shirt. "I love the way you look in your undershirt, all those muscles. Let me have them."

Now he was cursing bitterly as he carried her from the room. "You're going to pay for this. I swear. A hangover's going to be the least of it."

She giggled, kicking her legs, letting her hands run through his long, thick hair. She weighed next to nothing, but the muscles in his arms still began to quiver. His knees were going weak.

He nearly yelped when she bit his ear.

"Oh, I love this house. I love you. I love everything. Can we have wine in bed?"

"No, and you'd better—" He made the mistake of looking at her, and her mouth fused to his. Honorable or not, he was human. The heat ran through him, tormenting, tempting. With a long, desperate moan, he teetered on the stairs as he lost himself in those wonderful, willing lips. "Rebecca." Her name was a plea. "You're driving me crazy."

"I've always wanted to drive someone crazy. Then I could fix them, 'cause I'm a psychiatrist." Wiggling against him, she laughed uproariously. Her fingers tugged on the neck of the undershirt she'd uncovered, then snuck beneath, to flesh that was growing damp with sweat. "Kiss me some more, you know, the way you do when I can feel your teeth with my tongue. I just love when you do that."

"Oh, my God." As a prayer, it was perfectly sincere. He repeated it over and over again as he carried her to the guest room. It was his intention to dump her on the bed and make as quick and as dignified an exit as his scattered wits and aching loins would allow.

But she pulled, tugged, and had him flopping onto the big soft bed with her. On top of her. "Feels good." She sighed. Then arched. "Oh, my."

He moaned, pitifully. What was left of his mind scrambled so that all of the blood drained out of it, and down. He knew his eyes rolled back in his head when she latched those narrow hands on to his butt and squeezed.

"I'm not doing this." His breath was panting out with the effort to keep himself from ripping off her clothes.

"Are too. Soon as we get these pants off."

His hand vised over hers when she reached for the snap of his jeans. He stared at that glowing, cheerfully seductive face and, with a titanic effort, reminded himself there were rules to the game.

"I want you to stop this, right now." None too gently, he hauled her arms up over her head and pinned them. The only problem with that was that the position pushed his body more firmly to hers. And, damn her, she wouldn't keep still. "Keep your hands off me, damn it."

She grinned at him, lazily experimenting with the sensations that worked their way through her alcoholic haze whenever she rocked her hips. "I promise not to hurt you." A snort of laughter escaped. "You look so fierce. Come on and kiss me."

"I ought to strangle you." But he did kiss her, as much from frustration as from need. And the kiss was raw and wild and just a little mean. When he managed to pull himself back, her eyes were heavy and glazed. But those tempting lips curved.

"Mmmore…"

His body ached, his head throbbed. "You're going to remember when I make love with you, Rebecca," he said tightly. "You're going to be stone-cold sober, and you're going to remember every instant of it. And before I'm finished with you, you're not going to know your own name."

"Okay," she murmured agreeably as her heavy eyes drooped. "Okay." Then she yawned, hugely, and passed out.

He lay there several minutes, fighting for breath, fighting for strength. He could feel the steady rise and fall of the breasts that were crushed under him, the clean angles of her body, the limp droop of the hands he still held imprisoned.

"You're not going to hate me in the morning, baby," he muttered as he levered himself away. "But I might just hate you."

As an afterthought, he tossed a quilt over her, and left her fully dressed, right down to her shoes, to sleep it off.

He didn't sleep at all. As he had been all his life, Shane was up before the sun. But this morning he wasn't whistling. He did no more than glower down the hall toward Rebecca's room before he trooped downstairs and outside to begin the morning chores.

If the two 4-H students who worked with him on weekday mornings noticed he wasn't his usual cheerful self, they were wise enough to make no comment. Cows were milked and tended, pigs were fed, eggs were gathered. There were bales of hay to be split and spread.

The dogs danced around, as was their habit, but after a short time it seemed they sensed things were not quite as they should be. So they slunk off to lie low under the back porch.

The sun was up by the time Shane came back into the house to clean up and start his breakfast. Physical labor had helped work off most of his black mood. His sense of the ridiculous was dealing with the rest. Here he was, a grown man, he told himself, with a reputation for charming the ladies. And he was more frustrated than he'd been as a green adolescent taking that first tentative step into female territory.

It was laughable, if you looked at it from a little distance. Seeing the cool, sarcastic and quick-witted Dr. Knight wildly drunk was certainly worth the price of a ticket.

He thought about it as he fried up bacon. She'd certainly looked cute, sitting there with her glasses sliding off her nose and that stupid grin on her face. And a man couldn't complain overmuch about having a pretty woman wrap herself around him. No matter how frustrating it had been.

Of course, a different kind of man would have taken advantage of the situation. A different kind of man would have let her pull his clothes off, done the same courtesy for her. A different kind of man would have plowed right into that hot little body, and—

Because he was tormenting himself, he took several long, steadying breaths. She was damn lucky he wasn't a different kind of man. In fact, as he saw it, she owed him. Big.

That made him a bit happier as he poured himself a cup of coffee.

Then again, she was going to suffer plenty. As the smells of breakfast, the zing of caffeine, the simple beauty of the morning, worked on him, he decided he could even feel a little sorry for her.

She was going to wake up with a champion hangover and a lot of blank spaces. He was going to enjoy filling in those blanks, watching her cringe with embarrassment. It would even the scales somewhat. Enough, he thought, so that he could be compassionate. He'd give her some aspirin, along with the MacKade remedy for the morning after.

And if he got a couple of good laughs at her expense, well, she deserved them.

Poor baby, he mused, scrambling eggs briskly. She'd probably sleep until noon, then wake up, pull the covers over her pounding head and pray for a quick, merciful death.

All in all, it was a fair trade for the miserable night he'd spent.

He was very surprised when he turned the burner off under the skillet, reached for a plate and saw her standing in the kitchen doorway.

His brows lifted as he studied her. Definitely pale, he mused, heavy-eyed, still in her robe. Her hair was wet, which meant she'd probably tried to drown herself in the shower.

He grinned, just a little evilly.

"How's it going, Doc?"

Cautiously she cleared her throat. "Fine." She glanced toward the table. The evidence of her crime was still there. The bottle of wine, the glass still holding what she hadn't been able to gulp down. She was going to have to face it. "I guess I got a little carried away."

"You could say that." Looking forward to the next few minutes, he closed the cupboard door, perhaps a bit harder than necessary. She didn't wince at the bang, and that disappointed him. "Around here we'd say you were drunk as a skunk."

She did wince at that. "I'm not much of a drinker, as a rule. It was foolish, on top of an empty stomach. I want to apologize, and to thank you for getting me to bed."

His grin was rapidly fading. She was entirely too composed for his liking. "How's the head?"

"The head. Oh..." She smiled, relieved that he would care enough to ask. "Fine. I don't get hangovers. I must have a good metabolism."

He simply stared at her. Was there no justice? "You don't have a hangover?"

"No, but I could use some coffee."

She walked toward the pot. No stumbling, Shane noted as his resentment grew. No squinting away from the sunlight. Not even one quiet, pitiful moan.

"You drank the best part of a bottle of wine, and you feel fine?"

"Mmm... Hungry." She smiled at him again as she poured coffee. "I really was an idiot last night, and you were very understanding."

"Yeah." He was rapidly losing his appetite. "I was a brick."

He certainly had been, she mused, and he deserved an explanation along with her apology. "You see, I'd had this breakthrough, and..." The expression on his face warned her to fill in those details later. "You're angry with me. You should be. I was awful." She laid a hand on his arm. "Totally out of control. And you were so restrained and sweet."

"Sweet." He spit the word. "You remember what happened?"

"Of course." A bit surprised that he'd think she'd forget, she leaned back against the counter as she sipped her coffee. "I was—well, pawing you is the only way to describe it. Not my usual style. I'm very grateful you understood it was the wine talking. I wouldn't have blamed you for leaving me sprawled on the floor here.'' Because she was more amused at herself than embarrassed, her eyes laughed over her cup. ''I must have been quite a handful. I can't imagine a ridiculously drunk woman is very tempting, but you were very decent, very patient.''

She didn't even have the courtesy to be humiliated, he fumed. And, worse—much worse—she had the gall to make him into some sort of saint. ''You were obnoxious.''

''I know.'' Then she laughed and cut the last thread of his control. ''Still, it was an experience. I've never been so drunk—and don't think I care to be again. I was lucky I did it in private, and it was you who had to deal with me. Can I have a piece of this bacon?''

He was calm, he told himself, listening to the steady, if loud, beating of blood in his head. So he spoke calmly, quietly. ''Are you sober now, Rebecca?''

''As a judge.'' She nipped at a slice of bacon. ''And I'm going to stay that way for a long time.''

Slowly, he nodded, his eyes on hers. ''Head clear, all your faculties in order?''

She started to answer, but something in his tone tripped a warning bell. Warily she looked over at him. The dark, dangerous gleam in his eyes had her backing up a step. ''Shane—''

He yanked her back and sent the coffee cup she still held flying. ''So you weren't tempting?'' His mouth, full of fury and frustration, crushed down on hers. ''I was sweet?'' he added, swinging her around until her back rapped into the refrigerator. ''Understanding. Patient.'' Between snapped-off words, he continued to assault her mouth.

"Yes. No." How was she supposed to think, with all the blood roaring in her head?

"You damned near killed me." He jerked up her chin and plundered, shooting vicious spurts of fire into every cell of her body. "You know how much I wanted you? Get the picture?"

He gave her one, a very vivid one of hard, impatient lips, rough, ready hands, a body that was tight with tension and steaming with heat. She fought for breath, fought to stay upright as what was left of her mind went to mush.

She was melting against him again, soft, fragrant wax. His blood pumped in response to those soft, sexy sounds she made in her throat. Eager, helpless sounds that turned frustrated lust into a rage of desperate need.

"That's it," he muttered, and swung her up in his arms.

With a jolt of panic, she pushed a hand against his chest. "Wait."

"The hell I will." His eyes flashed at hers, all but searing her. "You'd better say no, loud and clear, and say it fast, Rebecca. Tell me you don't want me, don't want this. And make damn sure you mean it."

Under her palm she felt the furious beating of his heart, and her hand trembled. She'd thought it was fear, but it wasn't. Oh, no, it wasn't fear. It was longing.

"I can't." She let out a whoosh of breath. "I wouldn't mean it."

Triumph suited him. "I know."

Chapter Eight

She wanted to remember everything, to seal somehow every moment, every sound, every taste, into her mind and heart. She wanted to be able to recapture this incredible feeling of being carried in strong arms, of being wanted, and wanted with such ferocity, by a beautiful man. Of being sampled every few steps by skilled and hungry lips.

She didn't care if he was gentle or rough, patient or frenzied. As long as he didn't stop wanting her.

Then he paused on the stairs, his mouth swooping down on hers in a way that made any thought of the future float away to make room for the all-encompassing present.

On a moan of sheer delight, she wrapped her arms around him and let her own greedy mouth savor the taste of his face, his neck. The tangy flavor of him poured into her until her head swarmed with sound, revolved with half-formed images. The sheer force of her appetite made her shudder. This, she thought, dizzily, was only the beginning.

It no longer surprised her to find that her fingers were fighting with the buttons of his shirt. She wanted to feel him, touch him, everywhere, all at once.

He was out of breath and laughing by the time he made it to his own bedroom. "This is a lot like last night." He tumbled to the bed with her. On top of her. "Only better."

"Can't you get this thing off?" She was laughing, too, hadn't realized it was possible when desire was squeezing every throbbing inch of her body with sweaty fists.

"Yours is easier." With one expert stroke, he parted her robe. She was milk-pale, narrow of torso. With a low animal sound, he took her breast in his mouth.

The shock of it screamed through her, incited an avalanche of new and unexplored sensations. Even as she struggled to clear her mind to record them, the hands that had been busy on his shirt dropped away to grip frantically at the neat spread beneath.

Each tug, each nip, of his clever and hungry mouth shot arrows of golden heat straight to her center. Each arrow erupted into a dozen more flame-tipped missiles that streaked under her skin, over it, with dizzying speed.

How could anyone survive these sensations? she wondered. How could anyone live without them?

He had her naked in seconds, and feasted on her.

There was panic now—panic at the thought that it was possible to die from pleasure. Her skin was hot and damp, quivering at each pass and stroke of those big, callused hands. Tossed by a tidal wave, she rolled over the bed with him, desperate to keep up.

He couldn't get enough. All that baby-smooth skin, those long, narrow bones, the small, apple-firm breasts. He could smell her shower on her, and simple soap had never been so arousing. He thought he could eat her alive, bite by ravenous bite.

She was writhing under him, wrestling over him, her hands fast and frantic. Those wonderful eyes, the eyes he could never quite seem to get out of his head, were dark as whiskey now, and vividly intense. Everywhere he touched, she responded as though she'd never been touched before. Shuddering, arching, flowing. A purr, a moan, a gasp.

No woman he'd ever known had ever made him feel so powerful, so free, so needy.

"Damn it." Dizzy with desire, he sat up to drag at his boots. She reared up, wrapping that wonderful naked body around his, making his vision waver as she raced hurried kisses over his neck and shoulder.

"Hurry." She pulled up his undershirt and ravished his back. "Oh, I love your body. I just... Mmm..." She slid her breasts over the flesh she'd exposed and drove them both mad.

With an oath, he flipped her over into his lap. His mouth found hers waiting and avid. Her need, as wild as his, poured into him like a shot of raw whiskey.

To please them both, he cupped her, and she was hot and wet. He felt her body stiffen, tasted the warm rush of impact as her breath caught and expelled. She went wild, nails scraping, hips pumping, dazzling him with her unrestricted greed for pleasure.

"I've got to be inside you." His voice was harsh, his body frantic. Near violence, he shoved her back on the bed, yanked at his jeans. He couldn't remember his hands ever fumbling before, but they did now, in his outrageous and overwhelming rush to possess. "I want to fill you. I want to watch you take me."

"Hurry." Her hands were already gripping his hips. Oh, to feel like that again, to know he would send her flying again. "I can't stand it." She arched up to welcome.

He drove inside her, in one hard stroke. And froze. Shock, disbelief, terror, tangled with desperation when she cried out, when he felt himself ram mercilessly through her virginity. The muscles in his arms quivered from the strain, and his eyes, half-blind, locked frantically on hers.

"Rebecca. God. Don't move."

"What?" She was lost, delirious. Oh, the extraordinary feel of him inside her, inside her body, filling her with the sheer glory of invasion. "What?"

"For God's sake, don't move." He said it through gritted teeth as he fumbled for control. His body quivered on the tether he yanked ruthlessly to hold it in place. Sweet God, she was so hot, and tight, and wet.

"I'm not going to hurt you anymore." He couldn't get his breath, simply couldn't pull in enough air. "Just give me a minute."

"What?" she said again. With a primal instinct, she locked her legs around him and rose up.

"Don't—"

The animal took over, clawed aside everything but the urgent need to mate, and leaped free. Helpless to resist, he took her, plunging in deep, driving her to match his frenzied pace until the world seemed to contract to nothing but two bodies, linked. The hard slap of flesh on flesh, the explosive burst of air expelling from labored lungs, the musky smells of sweat and sex, and that glorious sensation of slicked bodies sliding. The dark pleasure swamped him, emptied him.

Weak, he collapsed on her and tried to gather his scattered wits. "I'm sorry" was all he could manage, and that was no more than a whisper. He had to move, knew he had to move, but he simply couldn't. No experience in his life had ever sapped him like this.

He told himself it was because she had been innocent and the guilt was draining him.

She was shuddering beneath him, quick, violent shudders that damned him. He was mortally afraid she was crying.

"Rebecca, you should have told me." There had to be some way he could soothe her, but this was simply beyond his experience.

"Told you?" she repeated, in a voice almost too faint to hear.

"I wouldn't have pushed you. I wouldn't have— Hell, I probably would have." He found the strength to ease back and look at her face. Her eyes were closed, her lips parted as the breath raced through them. "I hurt you. I must have hurt you."

Her eyes opened then. The gold was hardly more than a thin ring around the pupils. Shock, he thought, cursing himself again. But, to his confusion, those swollen lips curved.

"No, you didn't. It felt wonderful. I feel wonderful."

"But..."

"Does it always feel like that?" She let out a long, satisfied sigh. "So overwhelming, so... huge, as if nothing could stop you from getting from one incredible moment to the next. It's so..." She sighed again. "Primitive."

"I— No— Yes." What the hell was he supposed to say to that? To her? "I can't think straight yet."

Hearing that made her smile deepen. "I wasn't sure I'd be any good at it, but I was. Wasn't I?"

"You..." What the devil was going on? She wasn't crying, she wasn't upset at all. She looked like a cat who'd just dined on a platoon of canaries. More for his own benefit than for hers, he spoke slowly, carefully. "Rebecca, you'd never been with a man before."

"I wasn't particularly interested in a man before." She found the strength and started to lift her arms to circle him. Then her smile faded. "I wasn't good at it? I did something wrong? You're not feeling the way I'm feeling?"

"You destroyed me." Shane rolled off her to lie on his back and scrub his hands over his face. "I had no control. Even when I realized, I couldn't stop. I should have been able to stop."

"I'm sorry if I didn't do everything right." Stiff now with embarrassment, she sat up. "It was my first time, and I'd think you'd have some patience."

He swore at her and snagged her arm before she could climb regally from the bed. "Look at me. At me," he repeated, until her sulky eyes met his. "I'm not going to give you a damn grade, but I'll tell you this. I want you. Right now I want you again so much I could swallow you whole. It doesn't even seem to matter that I feel guilty that I was rough. If I'd known, I would have been gentle. I would have taken some care. I would have tried.''

''You didn't hurt me, Shane.'' Something in her heart shifted as she lifted a hand to his cheek. ''I didn't tell you because I thought it wouldn't happen if you knew. I thought you'd want someone with experience.''

''Who the hell are you?'' he murmured. ''Why can't I understand you?''

''I'm still working on understanding myself.'' Leaning forward, she touched her lips to his, then sighed as he drew her close to cuddle. ''This was the most beautiful first of my life. I want to feel this way again. You're an incredible lover.''

''How would you know?'' Surrendering, he nuzzled at her throat. ''Ah, Rebecca?''

''Hmm?''

''Is something wrong with those academic types? How'd they manage to let you get away?''

She rubbed her curved lips over his shoulder. ''If you'd known me even a year ago, you wouldn't ask. You wouldn't have looked at me twice.''

''I always look at women at least twice. Any woman.''

She chuckled, enjoying the feel of his muscles under her hands. ''I was a mess, believe me.'' It didn't sting to admit it now, not now that she nestled in his arms, still groggy from loving. ''A certified geek.''

Amused, he drew her back. ''Baby, no geek's ever had eyes like yours. I don't care what's in your brain, those eyes are pure sin.''

She blinked. ''They are?''

He laughed and hugged her hard. ''We're going to have to make love a lot. It dulls your wits.'' He tipped her head back, kissed her lightly. "I've got work that can't be put off, or we'd get started right now."

Testing, she slid her hands over his chest. "Can you work fast?"

His heart stuttered. Before they could get into trouble, he snagged her hands and lifted them to his mouth. "I think today I can work real fast."

She had work to do herself, but stayed where she was when Shane went downstairs. He would have to eat a cold breakfast, she mused, and found herself wonderfully smug at the knowledge that he'd hungered for her more than for food.

She'd tempted him. Destroyed him, she thought, grinning at the ceiling. His words. What a powerful, wonderful thing it was to be a woman.

As much as she would have loved snuggling in bed with him all morning, she was glad to have the time alone. Now she would be able to relive and savor every moment, every sensation, every surprise.

Dr. Rebecca Knight, prodigy, lifelong nerd, academic wonder and social oddity, had a lover women would kill for. And, at least for a little while, he was all hers.

With a throaty sigh, she lay back amid the tumbled pillows, holding the excitement, the wonder, to her.

He had the face of some dark, clever angel, the hands of a working farmer and the body of... Well, why be conservative? The body of a god.

And if you went beyond the surface—which was outstanding—he was kind and sweet. Volatile, certainly, but that only added to the package. He was sturdy, the kind of man who did what had to be done, who worked hard, loved his family, respected his roots, laughed at himself.

For heaven's sake, he even cooked.

In her estimation, he was as close to perfect as the species came. And wasn't it a fine stroke of luck that she should fall in love with perfection.

She reared up in bed with a jolt. That was a textbook reaction, she reminded herself, swallowing panic. She was mixing emotion with a physical experience. Enlarging affection and attraction into a complicated equation. It was a very typical female response. Sex equals love.

She knew better than that. She was a psychiatrist.

Very slowly, she lay back again. Intelligence, training, even common sense, had nothing with it. She laid a hand on her heart gingerly.

Of course she was in love with him. She'd been in love with him all along—the cliché of love at first sight. She'd ignored it, given it different names, fit her newly developed sophistication over it. But it had been there.

Well, what now? Not that long ago, she would have run like a rabbit. No doubt, if she greeted Shane with a declaration, *he'd* run like a rabbit. But wasn't it just one more new experience? An emotion to be added to the others she'd finally allowed herself to feel? The only sensible course of action was to accept it, and deal with whatever came next as best she could.

She had weeks left to enjoy what she could have, and enough experience to know how to live without what she couldn't have. It might hurt in the end, but she could accept that, too.

Much worse than pain, she well knew, was having nothing at all.

* * *

With the first days of September gleefully pouring out the last of the summer heat, Shane was sweaty when he headed for the house at midday. He was filthy, a little bloody where he'd scraped his knuckle on a bolt, and afraid he might smell a bit reminiscently of the manure spreader he'd just finished with.

But he'd also worked hard enough, and fast enough, to carve out two good hours of free time. He intended to occupy Rebecca for every moment of them.

He knew he had a stupid grin on his face, and didn't care. He wanted her in bed again, quickly. He needed to see if it had just been the novelty of her, or something more. All he was sure of was that he'd never been so involved, so lost in a woman, as he had been with her.

Because he'd never found it otherwise, he believed lovemaking was meant to be a pleasure. But with Rebecca, it had gone beyond pleasure, into delirium. He was looking forward to taking the trip again.

There she was at the table, working away, her glasses perched, long fingers flying. He started to grin, and a spear pierced his heart, painfully, when she looked up and smiled at him, her face lighting up.

"You really are beautiful," he murmured, and discovered he was clutching the doorknob for balance. Had a woman, any woman, ever knocked him off his feet before?

She could only stare at him. No one had ever called her beautiful. And at the moment, he looked as though he meant it. Then he grinned, and the dazed look left his eyes.

"Now, if you could only cook."

"I managed some iced tea."

"That's a start." And it might do something to cool his suddenly dry throat. He took out the pitcher, poured a generous glass and gulped. Choked. "Ah, how many bags did you use, Doc?"

"About a dozen."

He shook his head and hoped his eyes would stay in their sockets. The stuff in his glass was as thick and strong as a trucker's fist. "Well, it ought to get the blood moving."

She snickered. "Sorry. I'm useless in the kitchen. It probably shouldn't have steeped for three hours, either."

"Probably not." Cautiously he set the glass aside. He wouldn't have been overly surprised if it simply marched away under its own power. "We can dilute it. I've got a fifty-gallon drum outside."

"I could make a sandwich." When she rose, he held up a hand.

"Thanks anyway. I'll do it. No, don't come near me. I smell like the wrong side of a cow."

Enjoying the little bubbles of anticipation bursting in her blood, she traced her tongue over her lips. "You're awfully dirty," she said. She liked it. "And sweaty. Take off your shirt."

A lightning bolt of desire flashed into his gut. "You're very demanding. I like that in a woman." Still, he backed up again. "I don't want to touch you. You're all neat and tidy, and my hands are covered with things you wouldn't want on that pretty sweater."

She looked down at them, then let out a little hum of concern. "You're bleeding."

"Just scraped a knuckle. Let me wash up."

"I'll do it." She took his hand before he could turn on the tap.

She bathed his hand herself, knitting her brows over the scrape. He had the pleasure of standing there while she soaped his hands, rubbed them gently between hers.

He began to fantasize about taking a shower with her. Wet bodies, slicked skin, rising steam.

"I guess you'll live. But you should be more careful." She sniffed, wrinkled her nose. "What *have* you been doing out there?"

He grinned. "Spreading manure."

Her eyes popped wide. "With your hands?"

The intriguing little fantasy burst. He laughed so hard he thought his ribs would crack. "No, darling, we've got technology now, even out here in the boonies."

"Glad to hear it." She turned away, intent on helping him with his lunch, and bumped solidly into the refrigerator. "Damn it. I haven't done that in ages." Feeling ridiculous, she snatched her glasses off. "I used to forget I was wearing them and walk into things all the time."

He sent her a curious look. "I didn't think you forgot anything."

"Only about myself. Ask me about anything else, and I'll give you chapter and verse."

"Wool."

She turned and straightened, a platter of ham in her hand from the refrigerator. "Excuse me?"

"Maybe I'm thinking about buying some sheep. Tell me about wool."

"Don't be ridiculous."

He shrugged, reached for the bread. "I guess I found something you don't know about."

He didn't have to look to know her eyes had narrowed. He could hear it in her voice.

"An animal fiber forming the protective covering or fleece of sheep or other hairy mammals such as goats or camels. Wool is mainly obtained by shearing fleece from living animals. Cleaning removes the fatty substance, which is purified to make lanolin. Shall I go on?"

Amused, impressed, he studied her. "That's very cool. Where were you when I was in high school?"

"In a snooty boarding school in Switzerland, if my calculations are accurate."

"I imagine they always are," he murmured. The tone, the cool defense in it, told him this was something to be explored later. She spoke of boarding school the way he had once spoken of liver—as something highly detested.

"It's not just remembering facts," he said casually. "You obviously apply them. So how did you decide what to study?"

It was making her uncomfortable; she couldn't help it. However shallow and politically incorrect it might be, she preferred his interest in her body over his interest in her brain. "Initially, I was told what to study. My parents had a very specific blueprint for my education. Later, I concentrated on what held interest for me."

Her voice was cool and clipped, but he wasn't quite ready to let the subject go. He turned to get out the mustard. "You must have wowed your teachers."

She remained where she was, still holding the platter. "They were selected for their credentials in working with gifted children."

"My parents were relieved if I didn't get hauled down to the principal's office for a full week. Yours must have been thrilled with you."

"They're both very successful in their own right," she said flatly. "My father is one of the top vascular surgeons in the country, and my mother is a respected industrial chemist. They expected me to excel. Any other questions?"

Swampy ground again, he mused, sorry that he'd put that note of formality in her voice. He turned, looked at her, and was equally sorry he'd put that distant look in her eye. Just now, he wanted to see her smile again.

"Just one," he said. "What have you got on under that shirt?"

Relief loosened the muscles that had knotted her shoulders. "The usual."

"Oh, yeah?"

She did smile as she set the platter on the table. "Maybe you'd like to see for yourself."

"That's just what I had in mind."

She nipped around the far side of the table as he came forward. "After lunch."

His lips curved; his eyes danced. He looked wonderfully dangerous. "I don't want lunch."

He circled; so did she. "You have to keep your strength up, to spread that manure."

"I had a big breakfast. A big, late breakfast." He feinted, nearly snatched her, but she slipped away, laughing. "You're quick."

"I know."

He faked again and, as she pivoted, snaked out an arm to wrap around her waist. When he lifted her off her feet, she squealed with laughter. "I'm quicker."

It was dizzying to realize he could hold her suspended with one arm. Dizzying and exciting. "I let you catch me."

"Bull." He kissed her, hard, then tucked his other arm around her to swing her in three quick circles.

"You're making me drunk again." Laughing, she clutched at his shoulders and enjoyed the ride.

"Good." He swung her again, again, caught up in the joy of it, the joy of her. The sound of her laugh was thrilling, familiar. The feel of her body against his suddenly as vital as home...

"Put me down, you fool. John." Her head rolled back; the room spun. "Supper's burning."

She could smell it. The bottom of the pot would be scorched for certain. She could smell him—sweat and smoke and animal. Beneath her apron, the baby she carried quickened....

Panic and something else clogged Shane's throat. He set her on her feet, still supporting her as he shook her. "Rebecca. What is it?"

"It's happening again. Like last night." Her face was sheet-white, and her voice became faint and dreamy.... "There's stew in the pot, burning in the pot. Did you bring in more wood for the fire?" With her eyes unfocused, she pressed a hand to her stomach. "This one's a girl. Johnnie's going to have a sister...."

Then, as if a light had been switched on, her eyes cleared, sharpened. "My equipment." She broke away and raced to the living room. "Look at this! Just look. It's registering higher than last night. There's so much energy. I can feel it on my skin—like electric shocks."

While he watched, saying nothing, she began to mutter to herself, checking dials, gauges, monitors. All business now, her movements brisk and precise, she turned to her recorder.

"Event commenced at 13:20 and five seconds. Sharp sensory stimuli. Visual, olfactory." As if distracted, she ran a hand over her hair, then competently recounted everything that had happened.

"An overall sense of well-being," she finished, "of happiness. Love. It's possible sexual anticipation was caused by previous stimulation rather than the event, or was enhanced by previous stimulation." She tapped her finger on her lips, thinking. "End of event 13:24 and fifty-eight seconds, which at four minutes and fifty-three seconds makes it the longest to date."

On a long breath, she set the recorder down. "And the strongest," she murmured.

"Previous stimulation?"

She pulled herself out of her thoughts and turned to Shane. "I'm sorry, what?"

"Is that what you're calling it? Previous stimulation?"

"Technically." She dragged her hands through her hair again until it stood up in spikes. "That was incredible, absolutely incredible. Last night I was sitting in the kitchen, and I could see it change. It was smaller, and there was a fire in a little stone hearth, pies on the windowsill. There was a baby crying, Shane." Excitement sparkled in her eyes and seemed to shimmer in the air around her. "I got the baby crying on tape. I recorded it."

Pressing her hands to her cheeks, she laughed. "I could hardly believe it myself, even after I played it back half a dozen times. That's why I got out the wine. A little toast that turned into several big ones. I meant to tell you this morning, but we got distracted."

"Distracted."

Finally, the edgy tone of his voice, the flat look in his eyes, pierced through her exhilaration. The glow faded from her cheeks. He was pale, his face set, his eyes hard.

"Why are you angry?"

"Because this is nonsense," he tossed back, preferring anger to the heady sensation of fear. "And because I don't like being called a distraction, or a previous stimulation."

"That's not it at all."

"Don't you start on me. Keep your degrees in your pocket, and don't poke in my brain."

"You're not angry," she said quietly. "You're scared."

For an instant, his eyes were lethal. "I've got things to do."

She darted after him, grabbing his arm when they got to the kitchen. "You said you'd help me, Shane. You gave me your word on it."

"Leave it alone." Toughly he shook her off. "Leave me alone."

She simply stepped into his path and blocked it. Another man, she knew, might have mowed her down. And Shane had the temper for it, as well as the strength. But he also had what made him Shane.

"You had the same experience I did, felt the same things I did. I can see it in your face."

He reached out, picked her up and set her aside. "I said leave it alone."

"Who were John and Sarah?" She let out a breath when he stopped on his way to the door. "Her name was Sarah. Who were they, Shane? Who were we a few minutes ago?"

"I'm exactly the same person I am now as I was a few minutes ago. And so are you. If you're going to keep playing this game, leave me out of it."

"John and Sarah," she said again. "Was it John and Sarah MacKade? Would I find their names in your family Bible?"

He whirled back, stalked to the refrigerator. With one rigid hand, he jerked open the door, took out a beer. After twisting the top off violently, he tossed it aside and drank half the bottle down.

"My great-grandparents."

She let out a long, long sigh. "I see. And they lived here, in this house. They were the ones who tried to save the young Union soldier the day of the battle."

"So the story goes."

"What happened here just now—you've experienced similar things before."

He caught her quick look toward her computer and set his teeth. "No. No way in hell you're going to use me like some damn lab rat."

"All right, I'm sorry. This upsets you." She walked to him to run her hands up his arms. "But I think you need to know that for several years now I've had dreams. And now I know they were about this house, and those people."

He lowered his beer, but said nothing. Rebecca waited a moment, wondering if this kind of intimacy was more than either of them was prepared for.

"The dreams were one of the major reasons I began research into this field. They were—are—real, Shane. I've seen this room, this house, as it was more than a hundred years ago. And I've seen John and Sarah. I don't know if you have any old photographs of them to corroborate that. I can certainly describe them to you, at different periods of their lives here together. I can even tell you things she thought, felt, wanted. I think you can do the same with him."

"No." He said it flatly, finally. A lie for an honest man, a defense for a brave one. "I don't believe in any of that."

In frustration, she lifted her hands. "Do you think I'm making it up, that I'm making all of what just happened up?"

"I think you've got too many things crowded in that major-league brain of yours." To ease his hot throat, he took another swig of beer. "And I prefer reality."

She could have told him he was in denial, but that would only have made him angry—and possibly more resistant. Patience, she decided, patience and understanding, would be more productive all around.

"All right. We'll let it go, as long as you understand you can talk to me about it anytime."

"You're not my therapist."

"No, I'm not."

Her voice was entirely too reasonable. He slammed down the bottle. "I want you in bed, understand. That's what I want, that's what I need. Just you, just me." Grabbing her hand, he dragged her from the room. "Dreams are just dreams, and ghosts belong in bad movies. So you can just turn off that brain of yours. Distraction, my butt.''

He was all but heaving her up the stairs, and she felt twin sensations of alarm and arousal. "It wasn't meant as an insult.''

"Too many damn people inside you to suit me. I like it simple." He let her go to sit down on the edge of the bed and pull off his boots.

"I'm not simple," she said quietly. "Not the way you mean."

"This is simple." Boots dispatched, he rose to pull off his shirt, unhook his belt. "I want you. I break out in a sweat just thinking about you. That's basic, Rebecca. That's simple."

It was love, every bit as much as need, that had her moving to him, wrapping her arms around him. "I'm here." She lifted her head and drew his mouth down to hers.

She gentled him, as he would a skittish animal. Soothing hands, welcoming lips. He told himself that if this was familiar, this sinking into her, this allowing her to smooth away his worries, it was because he had lain with her here only that morning.

But as he fell into the sweet, seductive rhythm of loving her, it was as if there had been no one before, would be no one after. Only the texture of her skin would stay in his memory, the taste of her mouth, the sound of her sigh.

And as she rose to meet him in that fluid movement of comfortable sex, part of his mind fretted that he would never want, could never want, anyone else.

Even as he tumbled over that last edge of pleasure, he held himself back from a bigger, more dangerous fall.

Chapter Nine

I've now had three events at the farm. The last was during the night. I felt such grief, such tearing grief. There was a candle by the bed, burning. For a moment, I thought there was a figure standing by the window. Just standing, looking out at the night. While the grief was in me, it was also there, shimmering around that figure. A shared, yet separate, pain. I thought it was Shane, and started to get out of bed to go to him. But he was asleep beside me. And there was no one standing there at all.

I knew, clearly, that it was John and Sarah, and that their son was dead. I knew this even before Shane stirred restlessly beside me. He dreams, as I do, and he feels, as I do, but he doesn't want to speak of it. They're part of him, the people who lived here, who remain here in some fashion. Not only through blood, but through spirit. I wonder why they seem to be part of me, as well.

It upsets him, so I didn't tell him. Perhaps this is wrong. It's certainly unprofessional. But I'm learning that love has its own way. I love him so much, and in my own limited fashion would protect him from what haunts him.

I wonder what his feelings are for me, but I don't ask. I have to protect myself, as well. I can talk to him about anything but that. Anything at all. And I never run out of words. He's in the fields now. There is always so much work that must be done, yet he never seems to tire of it, or resent it. For myself, in this first, dizzying rush of love, I realize I could spend every second of every day with him and still not have enough time. It's a wonderful, liberating and humbling thing, this love. I'm so grateful I've had the chance to experience it.

If I could, I would take one moment, any single moment at all that I've had with him, crystallize it, preserve it, and carry it with me. Then, in all the years to come, I could take it out, not just to remember, but to relive.

Love gives you the oddest fantasies.

Rebecca heard the bark of the dogs, and the voices. Like a woman hiding a secret treasure, she saved her document and changed screens. Devin opened the door, followed by boys and dogs and all the noise that comes with them.

"Sorry. Didn't mean to bust in on you."

"That's all right." Automatically she lowered a hand to rub at the dogs, who came to greet her. "I was just finished."

"Cassie's just like the rest of the women in the county. Figures Shane must be starving." He set a dish on the counter. "She sent over an apple cobbler."

"It's great," Bryan informed Rebecca. "We had some of the other one she made already." Obviously at home, he poked into the refrigerator.

"Are you writing your book?" Connor approached more slowly, his eyes on her laptop.

"Not right now. Do you use a computer?"

He was studying hers with naked envy. "We get to use them in school sometimes. But they're not like this one."

"This one's loaded. Want to try it?"

He goggled. "Really?" He looked at his father, then put his hands behind his back. "I don't know how to work this kind."

"Nothing to it." Recognizing the look in his eyes, she laughed and took his hand to draw him closer. "I can show you. I've got everything backed up."

"Now you've done it," Devin murmured. "He's going to start pining for one."

"I can get you a deal on a used one." With a grin, she rose and pointed at her chair. "Sit down and give it a go. You must know the basic functions."

"Sure." The first thing he did was type his name. Connor MacKade.

"Does it play any games?" Bryan wanted to know.

"Nope. It's just a workhorse."

Losing interest immediately, Bryan cast his eyes on the cobbler.

"Forget it," Devin warned. "We came by to give Shane a hand with the haying," he told Rebecca. "You can expect the rest to descend before long."

"Oh." She glanced toward the window. "He's out there now, mowing it."

"Baling it," Devin told her. "First you mow, then you rake, then you bale."

"Right."

"You guys head out when you're done here. And don't pester Dr. Knight."

She followed him out to the porch and paused outside the door. "Devin, you lived here a long time."

"Most of my life."

"Have you ever had any unusual experiences? Of a paranormal nature," she added when he flashed a grin.

"You're asking if I think the place is haunted. Sure it is."

She shook her head. "You say that so casually."

"I've lived with it. You get used to it."

"Not everyone."

He followed her gaze to where Shane guided the tractor over the mowed hay. "Shane's got a stubborn streak."

"So I've noticed."

"And when it comes down to it, he's got a sensitive nature." Devin grinned again. "He'd bloody my nose for that one. But he does. Lived on a farm all his life, but he suffers if an animal's in pain, or if he loses one. Can't take it as a matter of course. There's a lot of leftover emotion in this house. It gets to him."

"Yet he lives here."

"He loves it," Devin said simply. "Every stone. Can you picture him anyplace else?"

She looked out to the hayfield again, smiled. "No. No, I can't. I could help him with what's here. If he'd let me."

"Maybe you could." Devin sighed. He was used to women falling for Shane, but it was easy to see that Rebecca was different. He doubted that she'd walk away unscathed when the time came. "I'd better go give him a hand."

She made some sound of agreement, and watched for some time before she went back into the house.

Devin told himself it wasn't his business as he walked across the field. In the easy rhythm of familiarity, he fell into step behind the baler. They worked together in silence until Shane shut off the motor.

"Rafe and Jared coming?"

"Should be on their way."

Shane nodded, squinted at the sky. "It's going to rain. We've only got another hour or two to get this in." But his gaze wandered to the house and stayed there.

"Damn it, Shane." Disgusted, Devin pulled out a bandanna and mopped his brow. "You're sleeping with her."

"Who?"

"Don't give me that. Aren't there enough women to dangle after around here without sniffing around Regan's friend? She's not even your type."

Shane worked to keep his temper in check. "You've always said I don't have a type."

"You know what I mean. That's a serious woman. Serious women have serious feelings. If she's not in love with you already, she will be. Then what the hell are you going to do?"

It cut just a little too close to the quick. Shane had always been careful to keep women from falling in love with him—seriously in love, in any case. And he knew he wasn't being careful with Rebecca.

"That's my business, isn't it? Mine and Rebecca's. I didn't push her into anything."

To drown out any more unwelcome advice, he cranked up the tractor again.

He wasn't going to talk about it, and he certainly wasn't going to worry about it. He meant to go on as he always had, and that meant, at this moment, getting the haying done before the rain hit.

He was grateful when the rest of his family showed up. It meant extra hands to load the hay wagon, drive it to the barn and off-load it. It also meant everyone was too busy working to pester him about his private life.

A man was entitled to a private life.

He cooled down considerably when it looked as if the job would be done before the storm hit. And when he could see children playing in the yard, dogs racing around and women going in and out of the house. Then there was the soothing quality of the steady vibration of the tractor under him, the voices of his brothers, that sweet, strong scent of hay. The clouds rolling in from the west shadowed the mountain, and the winter wheat he'd planted would welcome the rain.

In the kitchen, someone would be cooking, he mused, glancing over his shoulder to check the progress of the hay wagon. It wouldn't be Rebecca. She'd be playing with one of the babies. And when he walked in, covered with hay dust, she'd look over and smile.

She had the prettiest smile.

By the time they were hauling bales from wagon to barn, Shane had convinced himself that Devin was not only out of line, he was off base.

"So." Rafe took a break, gulping down some of the ice water from the cooler just inside the barn. "I didn't get a chance to talk to Rebecca. How's the ghostbusting?"

"She's into it." Sharp prickles of dry hay poked through his work gloves as Shane heaved a bale. "She gets pretty intense about something that's just a hobby."

"Hey, some people play golf," Jared commented, loading the hay lift.

"At least there's a purpose to that. Get the little ball in the hole, win the game."

"It's a puzzle to her," Jared added. "She strikes me as a woman who likes to solve puzzles, find answers."

"Maybe I'll buy her a jigsaw puzzle," Shane muttered.

"Bothers you, huh?" Amused, Rafe put his back into the work again. "Hear any chains rattling lately? Any disembodied moans?"

"Kiss my butt."

"How's it going otherwise?" Jared asked, with a vague thought to defusing an argument. Rain was beginning to patter on the ground, and they still had work to do. "Hasn't been a woman living in the house since Mom died. Cramping your style?"

A smile curved Shane's lips. "Nope."

"Well, hell." Catching Shane's look, Rafe set down the bale he'd just lifted. "You're sleeping with her."

"What am I, wearing a sign?"

"Can't you keep it in your pants for once?" In disgust, Rafe sliced his baling hook down. "Regan feels responsible for her."

Guilt and fear only inflamed a ready temper. "Why the hell should anybody feel responsible? She's a grown woman."

"You going to get that last load up here?" Devin called from the loft.

"Shut up." Shane spared him a glance before he turned on Rafe. "It's none of his business, it's none of your business."

"Anything connected to Regan's my business. And Rebecca's connected. What do you know about her? Do you know how she was brought up? How she spent all her time in classrooms, with tutors, in boarding schools?"

"What difference does it make?" Irritated because he didn't know, knew far from enough, Shane ignored the rain, the work, and let out the frustration on his brother. "She's got a brain, she uses it."

"That's all she was ever allowed to use. She wouldn't stand a chance if you aimed for her."

"What's the problem here?" Devin stepped out into the rain. "Are we going to get this load in before it's soaked, or just leave it?"

"Back off," Shane snarled at Rafe. "And stay out of my personal life."

Jared sighed. "Looks like we're going to leave it."

"This about Rebecca?" Interested now, Devin plucked out a spear of hay and gnawed on it. "We should've figured he'd hit on her."

"I didn't hit on her."

"That's bull. She'd barely unpacked her bags and you were stalking her in my kitchen. I should've punched you out right then."

Shane's eyes narrowed. "Try it now. You've got it all figured out, don't you? Now that you've got your pretty wife and your pretty kids. All of you." There was more anger than he'd realized boiling inside him. "I live my life my way, not yours. So stick your advice and your judgments and anything else you've got up your—"

From the kitchen window, Rebecca watched the four men. She was puzzled. At first it had seemed they were having some sort of serious discussion— some logistical problem with the hay, she'd concluded. Then it had looked as though an argument were brewing.

"Something's going on out there," she commented, and Savannah, an infant over her shoulder, wandered to the window.

"Oh, they're going to go at it."

"At what?"

"Each other, what else?" She shook her head and called to Regan and Cassie, who were busy at the stove. "Our boys are about to rumble."

"Fight?" Shocked to the core, Rebecca goggled. "You mean they're going to fight with each other? But why?"

Regan walked to the kitchen door, opened it. "It's just something they like to do from time to time."

"Do you think it's early enough to stop it?" Cassie wondered out loud.

"We can— No," Regan finished as the first blow was launched. "Too late."

With horrified eyes, Rebecca watched Shane's fist streak out and plow into Rafe's face. An instant later, they were rolling in the dirt. "But— But—"

"I'll make sure there's plenty of ice." Cassie turned away from the battle and went to the refrigerator.

"Why doesn't somebody stop them?" Regan demanded. "Jared and Devin are just standing there."

"Not for long," Savannah predicted.

As if on cue, Devin reached down. If his intention was to break it up, he failed miserably. Now there were three men wrestling in the mud the rain had churned up.

"This is ridiculous." By the time Rebecca reached the kitchen door, Jared had joined in the fray.

She couldn't see how any of them could tell who was fighting whom. She certainly couldn't. All she saw were arms and fists and bodies. All she heard were grunts and curses.

Outside of movies and television, she'd never actually seen anyone brawl. It was messier than she'd imagined, and certainly looked more painful.

"Isn't one of you going to do anything? They're your husbands."

"Well." Slowly Savannah ran a hand up and down Miranda's back. "We could put some money on it. I'll take Jared for five—it's a matter of loyalty."

"Five it is," Regan agreed. "Cassie?"

"All right—but Devin was up half the night. Ally's teething."

"No handicapping," Savannah declared. "Straight odds. You want to take Shane, Rebecca? Seems fair."

Totally baffled, she stared at the women. "Why, you're as bad as they are." She straightened her shoulders. "I'm going to put a stop to this, right now."

As Rebecca marched out, Savannah slanted a look at Regan. "To borrow Bryan's phrase, she's really stuck on him, isn't she?"

"I'm afraid so. It worries me."

"I think she's good for him." Cassie joined them at the door. "I think he's good for her, too. Both of them need someone, even if they haven't figured it out yet."

The only thing Rebecca figured as she marched toward the hay barn was that these four grown men—brothers, no less—were absolute fools.

By the time she neared the battlefield, she was soaked, her hair plastered to her head like a cap. She shook her head at the sight that met her eyes. The dogs had joined the party, racing around, occasionally leaping onto rolling bodies, then dancing away with delighted barks.

"Stop it." It halted the dogs, but not the men. Fred and Ethel sat politely, tongues hanging out, while the men continued to pummel each other. "I said stop this, right now."

Jared made the mistake of glancing over at the order and caught an elbow sharply on the chin. He retaliated by ramming a fist into the nearest belly.

Filled with righteous indignation, Rebecca slapped her hands on her hips. She didn't just hear grunts and curses now. They were laughing. Four baboons, she decided, laughing while they beat on each other.

She had a good carrying voice when she needed one. It had filled many a lecture hall. She used it now. "Stop this nonsense immediately. There are children in the house."

Devin paused, his filthy hand over Rafe's filthy face. "What?"

"Get up from there, all of you. You should be ashamed." Eyes hot, she scalded every one of them in turn. "I said get up. You." Choosing at random, she pointed a righteous finger at Devin. "You're a sheriff, for God's sake. You're supposed to uphold order, and here you are rolling in the mud like a hooligan."

"Yes, ma'am." Gamely he swallowed a chuckle and disengaged himself from the tangle of limbs. "Don't know what got into me."

"And you." That valiant finger aimed at Jared. "A lawyer. What are you thinking of?"

"Nothing." He rubbed a hand over his sore jaw before he rose. "Absolutely nothing."

"Rafe MacKade." She had the pleasure of seeing him wince. "A businessman, a pillar of the community. Husband and father. What kind of example are you setting for your children?"

"A poor one." He cleared his throat and got to his feet. He had the feeling that if he let the laugh loose she'd put him on his butt again.

"And you," she said, with such contempt in her voice that Shane decided to stay put in the mud. "I thought better of you."

"She sounds just like Mom," Shane murmured, and had his brothers nodding in respectful agreement. "Hey, I didn't start it."

"Typical response. Just typical. Is this how you solve your problems, your disagreements?"

He rubbed some of the dirt from his aching face. "Yeah."

"That's pathetic. You're all pathetic." Her authoritative look had three men shifting their feet and Shane grinning. "Violence is never the answer. There's no problem that can't be solved with reason and communication."

"We were communicating," Shane said, and earned a withering stare.

"I expect you to settle this like rational human beings. If you can't control yourselves, you'll just have to keep your distance from each other."

"Isn't she something?" Shane said, in a tone that had all three of his brothers studying him. "Have you ever seen anybody like her? Come on and kiss me, sweetie."

"If you think you can—" She let out a shriek as he swiped out a hand and had her sprawling on top of him. "You idiot. You brainless—"

Then she was flat on her back, covered by wet, hard male. His mouth, trembling with laughter, swooped onto hers. "She's the prettiest little thing."

He kissed her again, while mud oozed through her shirt.

"Get off me, you ape!" She bucked, wiggled and gave him a whack.

"Violence." He was shaking with laughter now, his battered, dirt-streaked face grinning down at her. "You see that?" he called out to his brothers. "She hit me. She isn't solving the problem with reason and communication."

"I'll communicate, all right." Her fist grazed his ear before his mouth fused to hers again.

And then he was kissing her senseless. The rain beat down, mud slicked her hands, and there was an audience of fascinated onlookers.

She just didn't care.

As he watched, Rafe found himself grinning. "I'll be damned," he murmured. "She's hooked him."

"I think you're right." Devin rubbed his bloody cheek on his muddy shoulder. "I've never seen him look at any woman that way. Think he knows it?"

"I don't think either of them have a clue." Delighted, Jared swiped wet hair out of his eyes.

"It's going to be a pleasure." Rafe hooked his thumbs in his pockets, rocking back on his heels. "A real pleasure, to watch Shane MacKade take the fall."

"Should we go inside and leave them alone?" Devin angled his head as he considered. "Or should we haul him off her and pound on him some more?"

Rafe touched his fingers to his eye. Shane's first punch had been a doozy. He was going to need some of the ice he was sure his wife was readying.

"I wouldn't mind pounding him some more, but she'd just get going again."

"I don't think we should leave them out here," Jared decided. "They could catch pneumonia."

"Not with all that heat." With a nod, Devin moved forward, and his brothers flanked him. Between them, they took arms and legs and hauled Shane into the air.

"Let go. You've got your own women. This one's mine." But they had him pinned, so he could only grin foolishly at Rebecca. "Baby, you're a mess. Let's go take a shower."

Eyes narrowed, Rebecca pulled herself to her feet. She knew she had mud in places best left unmentioned. With as much dignity as possible, she swiped her hands down her ruined slacks and through her filthy hair.

"Have you got him?" she asked calmly.

"Yes, ma'am." Recognizing the look in her eyes, Devin grinned. "I believe we do."

Shane knew the look, too, and tried to yank free. "Come on now, honey. Reason, remember? Violence isn't an answer. God, you're so pretty. I could gobble you right up. Why don't we—"

His breath whooshed out when she clenched a fist and rammed it into his stomach.

"Good one," he said weakly, then coughed and managed to draw another breath. "You show real potential."

"Idiot." With a toss of her head, she dripped her way to the house.

"Isn't she something?" Dazed with admiration and pain, Shane stared after her. "Isn't she just something?"

In the end, he tried flowers. After the chores were done, supper was eaten and his family had gone their separate ways, Shane calculated he needed a bit of an edge. He went out in the rain, in the dark, and picked wildflowers by flashlight.

When he came back, she was working at her computer. She did glance up; it was one of those cool, killing glances she'd aimed his way all evening.

He put the wet flowers on the table beside her and crouched down. "How mad are you?"

"I'm not angry." She was embarrassed, and that was worse.

"Want to hit me again?"

"Certainly not."

"It was just mud." He took her hand, brought it to his lips. "It looked good on you."

She would have tugged her hand away, but he was nibbling on it. "I'm trying to work."

"Wasn't the term you used *avoidance?*" When she turned her head to glare, he picked up the flowers and held them out. "I'm crazy about you."

She let out a sigh. What was so important about dignity, anyway? "You must be crazy to go out on a rainy night to pick flowers."

"It always worked with my mother. You reminded me of her today, when you were letting us have it. Of course, she'd have pulled us up by the scruff of the neck, and then lectured. I guess we were smaller then."

Unable to resist, Rebecca sniffed at the dripping blooms. "She must have been quite a woman."

"She was the best," Shane said simply. "They don't come any better. She and my father, well, they were terrific. You always knew somebody was there, ready to give you a kick in the butt or a helping hand, whichever you needed most." Reaching up, he stroked a finger over her cheek. "I guess that's why I don't really understand loneliness."

"Big families aren't always a buffer against it. It's the people in them." She scraped back her chair. "I'd better put these in water."

She wasn't going to tell him, he realized. She wasn't going to speak of her background, her family, unless he pushed. "Rebecca—"

"What were you fighting with your brothers about?" She asked it quickly, as if she sensed what he'd been going to ask.

"Stuff." Then he shrugged. If he wanted her to be honest, he had to be, as well. "You."

Stunned, she turned back. "Me? You're joking."

"It wasn't a big deal. Rafe said something to tick me off. That's usually all it takes." He crossed over, bent down to take a slim old bottle out of the bottom cupboard. "They think I'm taking advantage of you."

"I see." But she didn't. She took the bottle, filled it, then began to carefully arrange the flowers. "You told them we were intimate."

"I didn't have to." He had an idea of what she was imagining. Locker-room talk, snickers, bragging and nudging elbows. "Rebecca, I didn't talk about what's between us."

And he might have, probably would have, he realized, if it had been another woman. Frowning, he walked over to pour coffee he didn't want.

He didn't go around bragging about his relationships with women. But with his brothers, he would certainly have made some comment about a new interest. He'd kept his feelings about Rebecca to himself.

And it wouldn't have bothered him in the least to have Rafe or any of the others tease or prod about his exploits with a woman. Yet it had with Rebecca. It had hurt and infuriated and—

"What the hell is this?" he muttered.

"I thought it was coffee."

"What?" He stared into his mug. "No, my mind was wandering. Look, it wasn't a big deal. It's just the way we are. We fight." He smiled a little. "We used to beat on each other a lot more. I guess we're mellowing."

"Well." Thoughtful, she carried the flowers to the table, set them in the center. "I've never had anyone fight over me before—especially four big, strong men. I suppose I should be flattered.''

''I have feelings for you.'' It came right out of his mouth, out of nowhere. Shaken, Shane lifted his mug and gulped down coffee. ''I guess I didn't like the idea of somebody thinking I'd pushed you into bed.''

Warmth bloomed inside her. A dangerous warmth, she knew. A loving one. She made certain her voice was light. ''We both know you didn't.''

''You haven't exactly been around the block. I wanted you. I went after you.''

''And I put up a hell of a battle, didn't I?''

''Not especially.'' But he couldn't smile back at her. ''I've been around the block, a lot of times.''

''Are you bragging?''

''No, I—'' He caught himself. There was amusement in her eyes, and understanding, and something else he didn't know quite what to do with. ''I guess what I'm trying to say is that I'd try to go along with it if you wanted to rethink the situation, or take some time.''

She swallowed a nasty ball of fear. Fear made the voice tremble, and she wanted hers to be steady. ''Is that what you want?''

With his eyes on her, he shook his head slowly. ''No. Lately I can't seem to want anything but you. Just looking at you makes my mouth water.''

The warmth came back, pulsed, spread. She crossed the room, lifted her arms to twine them around his neck. ''Then why don't you do more than look?''

Chapter Ten

There were many places to talk to ghosts. An open mind didn't require a dark night, howling winds or swirling mists. This day was bright and beautiful. Trees touched by early fall were shimmering in golds and russets against a sky so blue it might have been painted on canvas.

There was the sound of birdsong, the smell of grass newly mowed. There were fields crackling with drying cornstalks, and, like a miracle, there was a lone doe standing at the edge of the trees, sniffing the air for human scent.

Rebecca had come to the battlefield alone. Early. She lingered here, near the long depression in the ground known as Bloody Lane. She knew the battle, each charge and retreat, and she knew the horrid stage of it when men had fallen and lain in tangled heaps in that innocent-looking dip in the land.

There was a tower at the end of it, built long after the war. She'd climbed it before, knew the view from the top was glorious. From there, she would be able to see the inn, the woods, some of Shane's fields.

But it didn't call to her as this spot did. Here, on the ground, there was no lofty distance between the living and the dead.

She sat down on the grass, knowing she would feel only a sadness, an intellectual connection with the past. As compelling, as hallowed, as the ground was, she could only be a historian.

Ghosts didn't speak to her, not here. It was the farm that held the key for her. The farm that haunted not only her dreams now, but her waking hours, as well. She accepted that. But what was the connection there? What was the emotional link? A link so strong it had pulled at her for years, over thousands of miles.

That she didn't know.

She knew only that she was in love.

She lifted her face to the breeze, let it run its fingers through her hair as Shane often did. How could she be so content, and yet so unsettled? There were so many questions unanswered, so many feelings unresolved. She wondered if that was the way of love.

Was she still so passive, so undemanding of others, that she could settle so easily for what Shane offered? Or was she still so needy, so starved for love, that she fretted for more when she had enough?

Either way, it proved that a part of her, rooted deep, hadn't changed. Perhaps never would.

He cared for her, he desired her. She was pathetically grateful for that. He'd be shocked to know it, she was certain. She would keep that to herself, just as she kept this outrageous and overwhelming love for him to herself.

She had plenty of practice at restricting and restraining her emotions.

Common sense told her she was being greedy. She wanted all the love, the passion, the endurance, that lived in that house for herself. She wanted the stability of it, the constancy, and the acceptance.

She was the transient, as she had always been.

But she wouldn't leave empty-handed this time, and that thought soothed. There wouldn't simply be knowledge received and given, there would be emotion—more emotion than she had ever received, more than she'd ever given. That was something to celebrate, and to treasure.

That should be enough for anyone.

Sitting alone, she gazed over the fields, the slope of the hill, the narrow trench. It was so utterly peaceful, so pristine, and its beauty was terrible. She'd studied history enough to know the strategies of war, the social, political and personal motivations behind it. Knew enough, too, to understand the romance that followed it.

The music, the beat of the drum, the wave of flags and the flash of weapons.

She could picture the charge, men running wildly through the smoke of cannon fire, eyes reddened, teeth bared. Their hearts would have pounded, roaring with blood. They had been men, after all. Fear, glory, hope, and a little madness.

That first clash of bayonets. The sun would have flashed on steel. Had the crows waited, nasty and patient, drawn by the thunder of swords and boom of mortar?

North or South, they would have raced toward death. And the generals on their horses, playing chess with lives, how had they felt, what had they thought, as they watched the carnage here? The bodies piling up, blue and gray united by the stain of blood. The miserable cries of the wounded, the screams of the dying.

She sighed again. War was loss, she thought, no matter what was gained.

Always there would be a John and Sarah, the essence of the grieving parents for dead sons. War stole families, she reflected. Cut pieces out of hearts that could never truly heal.

So we build monuments to the wars, and the dead sons. We tell ourselves not to forget. John and Sarah never forgot. And love endured.

It made her smile as she rose. The grass was green here, and the air quiet. She decided that the world needed places of loss to help them remember what they had.

She went home to write.

It was nearly time for evening milking, Rebecca realized, and she laughed at herself. How odd that she would begin to gauge the day by farm chores. With a shake of her head, she hammered out the next sentence.

Why had she spent all her life writing technical papers? she wondered. This flow of emotion and thought and imagination was so liberating. Damned if she didn't think she might try her hand at a novel eventually.

Chuckling at the thought, she tucked it into the back of her mind. There were plenty of people who would consider her present topic, the supernatural, straight fiction.

When the phone rang, she let the next thought roll around in her head as she rose to answer. Absently she reached for the coffeepot and the receiver at the same time.

"Hello?"

"Dr. Rebecca Knight, please."

She stiffened, then ordered herself to relax. Why should it surprise, even annoy her, that her voice hadn't been recognized? "This is Rebecca. Hello, Mother."

"Rebecca, I had to go through your service to track you down. I assumed you were in New York."

"No, I'm not." She heard the door open and worked up a casual, if stiff, smile for Shane. "I'm spending some time in Maryland."

"A lecture tour? I hadn't heard."

"No, I'm not on a lecture tour." She could easily visualize her mother flipping through her Filofax to note it down. "I'm . . . doing research."

"In Maryland. On what subject?"

"The Battle of Antietam."

"Ah. That's been covered very adequately, don't you think?"

"I'm coming from a different angle." She made way so that Shane could get to the coffee, but didn't look at him. "Is there something I can do for you?"

"Actually, there's something I can do for you. Where in the world are you staying, Rebecca? It's very inconvenient that you didn't leave word. I need a fax number."

"I'm staying with a friend." She turned her back, avoiding Shane's eyes. "I don't have a fax here."

"Surely you have access to one. You're not in the Dark Ages."

Now she did glance at Shane. He smelled of the earth, and carried a good bit of it on his person. "Not exactly," Rebecca said dryly. "I'll have to check on that and get back to you. Are you in Connecticut?"

"Your father is. I'm at a seminar in Atlanta. You can reach me through the Ritz-Carlton."

"All right. Can I ask what this is about?"

"It's quite an opportunity. The head of the history department at my alma mater is retiring at the end of this semester. With your credentials and my connections, I don't see that you'd have any difficulty getting the position. There's talk of endowing a chair. It would be quite a coup, given your age. At twenty-four, I believe you'd be the youngest department head ever placed there."

"I was twenty-five last March, Mother."

"Nonetheless, it would still be a coup."

"Yes, I'm sure it would, but I'm not interested."

"Don't be ridiculous, Rebecca."

She closed her eyes for a moment. That tone, that quick, dismissive tone, had whipped her along the path chosen for her all her life. It took a hard, wrenching effort for her to stand her ground.

"I'm afraid I'll have to be." And where had that cold, sarcastic voice come from? Rebecca wondered. "I don't want to teach, Mother."

"Teaching is the least of it, Rebecca, as you're quite aware. The position itself—"

"I don't want to be the dean of history, or the history chair, anywhere." She had to interrupt quickly, recognizing the old, familiar roiling in her stomach. "But thank you for thinking of me."

"I'm not happy with your attitude, Rebecca. You are obligated to use your gifts, and the opportunities your father and I have provided for you. An advancement of this stature will make your career."

"Whose career?"

There was a sigh. Long-suffering. "Obviously you're in a difficult mood, and I can see that gratitude won't be forthcoming. I'll depend on your good sense, however. Get me your fax number as soon as possible. I'm a bit rushed at the moment, but I'll expect to hear from you by the morning. Goodbye."

"Goodbye, Mother."

She hung up and smiled at Shane brightly, overbrightly, while the muscles in her stomach clenched and knotted. "Well, cows all bedded down?"

"Sit down, Rebecca."

"I'm starving." Terrified he would touch her and she would fall apart, she moved away. "I think there's still some of that chocolate cake one of your harem dropped off."

"Rebecca." His voice was quiet, and his eyes were troubled. She kept pressing a hand to her stomach, he noted, as if something inside hurt. "I think you should sit down."

"I can make more coffee. I've figured this thing out." She started to reach for the canister, but he stepped forward, took her shoulders gently. "What?" The word snapped out, her body jerking.

Careful, he thought, disturbed by the brittle look in her eyes. "So, you're from Connecticut."

She hesitated, then shrugged her shoulders under his hands. "My parents live there."

"That's where you grew up."

"Not exactly. I lived there when I wasn't in school. You don't want to drink that," she added, glancing at the pot. "It's been sitting for hours. I'd said I'd make fresh."

"What did she say to upset you, baby?"

"Nothing. It's nothing." But he kept holding her, kept looking at her with boundless patience and concern. "She wants me to campaign for a position at her college. It's a very prestigious position. I'm not interested. It's a divergence of opinion, and she's not used to me having an opinion."

It was simple enough, he thought, or it should have been. But there was nothing simple about her reaction. "You told her no."

"It doesn't particularly matter. It never did, on the rare occasions I actually got up the courage to say it. I expect my father will be calling shortly, to remind me of my obligations and responsibilities."

"Who are you obligated to?"

"To them, to education, to posterity. I have a responsibility to use my talents, and to reap the rewards. It's just a variation on 'Publish or Perish,' the battle cry of academia. Let's forget it."

He let her move away, because she seemed to need it. Her hands were steady as she measured out coffee, and her face was blank while she filled the pot.

Then, with a shudder, she set everything down. "I can't believe I'm doing this. This is how I got ulcers."

"What the hell are you talking about?"

"Ulcers, migraines, insomnia, and a near miss with a breakdown. Isn't this why I studied psychiatry?"

She wasn't talking to him, Shane realized, so he said nothing. But he was beginning to burn inside.

"Repression isn't the answer. I know that. It's one of the things that punish the body for what's closed up in the mind. It's always so much easier to analyze someone else, always much harder to see things when it's yourself."

Her rigid hands raked through her hair. "I'm not going to be directed this time. I'm not going to be hammered at until I give. The hell with them. The hell with them. They never did anything but make me into a miserable, neurotic freak."

She whirled back to him. Her face wasn't blank now, it was livid. "Do you know what it's like to be four years old and expected to read Dante in Italian, and discuss it? To sit at the dinner table, when you weren't shuffled off somewhere else, and be quizzed on physics or converse about the Renaissance—in French, naturally?"

"No," he said quietly. "Why don't you tell me what it's like?"

"It's horrible. Horrible. To have your own parents regard you as a *thing,* a rousing success of genetics. I hated it, but what choice do you have when you're a child? You do what's expected of you. Then you get in the habit and you keep right on doing it even when you're not a child. One day you look in the mirror, and you see something so pathetic it hurts to look. And you wonder, why not just end it?"

The anger inside him turned to dry-mouthed shock. "Rebecca."

Impatient, she shook her head. "Maybe you fantasize about it, even obsess. And you're clever, you're so damned clever that you can find the most effective, the most painless way, to accomplish it. And, of course, the most tidy."

He didn't speak now. She'd shaken him down to the bone, and he was chilled to the marrow. This woman, this beautiful, precious woman, had considered ending her life.

She rubbed absently at the headache that throbbed dead-center in her forehead. "But you're too intelligent, too well programmed, to tolerate that kind of waste. It frightens you a little to realize you could actually do it, so you decide—being a practical person—to study human behavior, psychiatry, instead. A much more productive outlet, all in all."

"How old were you?" he managed, but had to take a steadying breath before he could go on. "How old were you when you..."

"Researched suicide?" she said calmly. "Twelve. A dangerous age, all those hormones to deal with. A shock to the regimented system. You have to remind yourself that life, however miserable, is all you've got, and go on with it. It's easier to go on with it if you just close up, close off, lock yourself behind books and theories, credentials and degrees. Until you realize that's just a different kind of suicide."

She took a long, shuddering breath. "I'm tired," she murmured, rubbing her hands over her face. "They make me so tired."

Ulcers, a breakdown. Dear God, suicide. What the hell had they done to her? He wanted to tear them apart. All of them. Any of them who had ignored her heart to get to her mind. He wanted, desperately, to go back in time and find that young girl, to give her everything she'd needed and deserved.

But he could only reach out to the woman.

"Come on." He went to her, held her, close and gentle, despite the storm raging inside him. She needed his calm, not his fury. "Just lean on me awhile."

"I'm all right."

"No, you're not. But you will be." He damn well would see to it. "Hold on to me, baby."

So she did, and it was so easy. "She didn't do anything wrong, not really. We haven't seen each other in more than a year. I doubt she or my father would recognize me if we passed on the street. The change would surprise them."

He rubbed his cheek over her hair. She felt so fragile. Why hadn't he seen that before? Where hadn't he looked to see this hurt, vulnerable side of her?

"It doesn't matter what they think, only what you want."

"You can't always have everything you want. Once I wanted them to love me. I'd have done anything if they'd just said they loved me. You know the problem with a memory like mine? You can't forget things—even when you want to. I remember when they first sent me to boarding school. I was so frightened, so lonely and unhappy. They put me on a plane, didn't even go with me. I was six years old."

"Oh, baby, I'm so sorry."

"They could see I had an adult mind, but they never considered the child's heart. Well, I'm grown-up now. I should handle it better."

"You're handling it fine."

"Not fine, but better." She eased back a little. "I'm sorry. If you'd come in an hour later, I'd have been over it."

"I want you to tell me what you feel." Very gently, he lowered his head and touched his lips to hers. "I want to know who you are, and how you got there. I haven't been able to figure you out, Rebecca. All those different pieces of you that never quite seem to fit. Now they're starting to. Do me a favor?''

''What?''

''Don't call her back. Let her stew.''

She smiled a little. ''That's rude.''

''Yeah. So?''

''She'll just call again. My father will call. They—'' To prove her point, the phone rang. ''There you are.''

He tightened his grip before she could move. Nothing was going to put that shattered look back on her face while he was here to protect her. ''I don't hear anything.''

''The phone.''

''We don't have a phone.'' Thinking only to give her peace, he kissed her again. And brought himself some, as well. ''And we're not here, anyway.''

''Where are we?''

He scooped his arm under her knees, picked her up. ''Anywhere you want to go.'' As the phone continued to shrill, he carried her out of the room. ''As long as it takes a real long time to get there.''

When he reached the bedroom, he set her on her feet. The phone had stopped ringing, and he took it off the hook, then set the receiver in a drawer to muffle the buzz.

''That ought to do it.''

''You don't even have an answering machine. It'll drive them crazy.''

''Good.'' He'd have liked an opportunity to speak to either of her parents himself. But that could wait. At the moment, he had only one priority, and that was erasing the troubled look in Rebecca's eyes. "So, where do you want to go?"

She shook her head, her smile puzzled. "I thought we were there."

"This is just the starting-off point." He ran a finger down the vest she wore over a mannish shirt. "A tropical island? A—what do you call it?—mountain chalet? We could be snowed in. A castle, maybe." He brushed his lips over her brow. "Let's pretend."

"Fantasizing is often a—"

His lips slid down to hers. "Let's pretend. A long, empty beach, white sand, palm trees. Smell the flowers." Gently he kissed her eyes closed. "Hear the surf. Let's go there. I love the way your skin looks in the moonlight." He nibbled at her lips as he slipped the vest aside and slowly, so slowly, undid the buttons of her shirt. "There's moonlight on the water, on you. Pretty Rebecca." Lightly he cupped her breasts. "Come away with me."

"Anywhere," she murmured, and let him take her.

"There's no one but us." He drew off his shirt, always keeping contact with his mouth, on her lips, her cheek, the curve of her ear. "And nothing to do but make love. I want to make love with you, Rebecca. Only you, Rebecca. Day and night."

The words were seducing her. Words were powerful, she knew, and his were captivating her. His skin was under her hands now, wonderfully smooth and warm. His heart beat slow and thick against hers. She would have sworn she heard the waves hiss and rise on the sand.

"In the surf," she said dreamily as those wonderful hands glided over her. "With the water flowing up, then away."

"That's right. Your skin's wet and cool. Slick," he said as he continued to undress them both. "And it tastes of salt." Still murmuring, he lowered her to the bed. "There's starlight in your eyes." He could see it, though the last rays of the sun slanted through the windows. "Silver sparkling in the gold. We can stay as long as you like. As long as you want."

His mouth slid over hers, coaxing, giving, taking just a little more when her lips softened on a sigh. Beneath his, her body was soft, yielding, surrendering. She was with him now, he knew. Pulse to pulse. He wanted to show her what it was to be cherished.

So his hands were gentle, his lips tender, and each move, each shift, was fluid and patient. Loving. He lingered where he knew it pleased her most, going quietly, easily, sinking a little deeper with each stroke of his hands into the fantasy he'd created for her.

She was floating. It could have been water sliding over her, so sensitive were his hands. And the gift he brought to her was a liquid yearning as much of the soul as of the body.

She dreamed there was sand beneath them, wet and smooth. And the wind at the windows was the musical murmur of surf. The dim light seemed to be rich and silver with the full, rising moon. The exotic perfume of island flowers, the midnight sea that stretched forever, the romantic song of tropical birds.

And her lover was there, holding her.

"Where are you, Rebecca?"

"With you."

"Stay with me."

She wrapped her arms around him.

He loved her endlessly, building the pace, letting the current take her up, over. When she tumbled down, he was there to catch her, to begin the journey all over again. Knowing she was lost in him, in them, was the most exciting thing he'd ever experienced. Each sigh, each moan, each catch of her breath, poured through him like wine.

Whispering her name, he drew her up until they were torso to torso and the pace had to quicken or he would go mad. He found her breasts, drawing them hard into his mouth when she arched back. When she cried out his name, it was like music, with a driving beat that burned in the blood.

He had shown her she was cherished. Now he would show her she was craved.

All she could think was that the storm was coming.

Now it was wild, windy, and the waves lashed against her, threatening to drag her under, into the swirling dark. And she would go, willingly, as long as she could stay with him. So, she clung to him, her mouth desperate on his, her body straining toward each shattering fall. She plunged her hands into his hair, took greedy handfuls of it when he lifted her up to race lips and teeth down her body.

She was drowning, and glorying in it. From some dim corner of her mind, she heard her own voice begging him for more.

The moonlight was gone. Now there was only the flash of lightning, the bellow of thunder. Still he held her up, assaulting her system, destroying her nerves. She could feel the muscles in his arms quiver when he shifted. And he was under her.

"Look at me." His voice was rough, raw, his fingers dug deep in her hips. "Look at me. I want to see your eyes."

She opened them, and through her wavering vision saw his face. It was tensed, strained. Beautiful. "Come inside me. Now, for God's sake, Shane. I need you."

"Who are you?"

"Yours," she said, then cried out when he lowered her onto him.

She couldn't breathe, was sure her heart had stopped. Her body curved back like a pulled bowstring. Staggered, undone, she stroked her hands up her own quivering body, from belly to breasts, then up over her hair, where they linked as if to anchor her.

He'd never seen anything more beautiful, more arousing, more exciting, than Rebecca lost in pleasure. He watched her head fall back, saw the intensity of the climax that ripped through her. To savor the moment, he held himself still, let her absorb every instant of that first assault of sensation.

Then she began to rock, and that rhythmic demand spurred him to match it. Faster, until speed was all that mattered. When he could no longer wait for her, he clutched her hands, took her, and dragged her under with him.

When his mind cleared a little, he realized that the sun had set and the room was soft with shadows. And that he had never in his life felt more content.

He waited until she lay still, her body sprawled limply over his, her breathing almost steady.

"So, where do you want to go now?"

Her laugh started out low in her throat, then rumbled out, the way he liked it best. "Why don't we try that mountain chalet? Snow would be a nice change of pace."

"Good thinking. After dinner, we can—"

"After dinner, hell." Eyes wicked, she lifted her head and began to nibble on him.

"Ah, listen, baby, I..." His breath hitched when she slid down and scraped her teeth over his nipple. "Maybe if you could give me a few minutes to..." Her hand slid lower, much lower. His oath was soft, reverent.

"You've got a reputation to uphold," she murmured, deciding she liked the idea of playing seductress with an exhausted man. "I've heard around town that you're... let's say insatiable."

"Yeah, well. People exaggerate. A little." Ten minutes, he thought. No, five, he told himself, watching her neat, narrow, naked body slither over his. He just needed five minutes to recover. "Listen, why don't we— Man, you're getting good at that."

She looked up, laughing, thrilled with herself. "I have a photographic memory, in case you've forgotten, and a very quick mind."

"You're telling me. Anyway, why don't we take a shower, or maybe a little nap? I don't think I'd be much good to you at the moment." He gulped in air when her busy mouth trailed lower. He wondered if his eyes crossed. "Then again, maybe I could handle it after all."

"I think we can count on it."

They did take a shower, later. She watched Shane stick his head under the spray and groan in appreciation. From behind, she wrapped her arms tight around him and pressed her mouth to his wet back.

"Jeez, woman, do I look like a rabbit?" But he turned to her, always willing to try.

"No." Laughing, she lifted her hands to his streaming hair. "That was to thank you."

"Okay." He dumped shampoo on her hair and scrubbed. "For what?"

She blinked as lather dripped, stinging, into her eyes. "You must have been tired and hungry when you came in. But you wanted to take my mind off things."

"Yeah, it was a hardship, all right. I don't know how I got through it." Amused, he nudged her under the spray.

"I mean it." She sputtered, tried unsuccessfully to wipe her eyes. "You were wonderful. I'll never forget it."

"That's what they all say." He grinned when she turned and gave him a narrow-eyed stare. "Kidding."

"You know, of course, that most accidents in the home occur in the bathroom."

"I've heard that. Gotta watch your step."

"Watch yours."

He put his hands on the tile and boxed her in. "Remember the first time we made love in here? Sure you do, you don't forget anything."

She lifted her brows. "You're not going to distract me that way."

"I could if I wanted." He lowered his mouth to hers. "But if I don't eat, I'm going to fall down."

"How about if I make you soup?"

He looked pained. "Do you have to?"

She sniffed, ducked under his arm and stepped out of the stall. "Cook your own dinner then."

"You know what I've noticed?" Casually he turned off the shower, reached for a towel. "You pick up things in a snap. I mean, you ask a million questions, figure it out, file it all away. I'd bet you could go out there in the morning and handle the milking without a hitch.''

"Don't get any ideas," she warned him, and toweled off, then bundled herself into a robe.

"I've seen you work a crossword puzzle in something under two minutes. That time we went to the market and you bought groceries, you had the money out before the total came up. To the penny."

She shrugged, picked up a comb from the side of the sink and ran it through her hair. "So, I'm good at parlor tricks."

"You could probably build a nuclear reactor in the living room if you put your mind to it. But you can't fry an egg." Watching her, he wrapped the towel around his hips. "Or, more accurately, you don't want to fry an egg, so you don't bother to figure it out."

She flicked a glance over her shoulder. "Caught me. Now what's your point?"

"I'll cook, and you build the nuclear reactors."

She smiled, but he saw the hint of clouds in her eyes. "Rebecca." Patient, he cupped her face in his hands. "Your brain is only one of the very appealing things about you. I like watching you think almost as much as I like watching you when you can't think. Whatever it took to get you to this point doesn't matter. Because you're here."

She let out a sigh. "It's hard to stop wishing you could be normal."

"Baby, you are normal. It doesn't mean you can't be special."

That was so simple, she thought. And so sensible. And so like him. Rising on her toes, she touched her lips to his. "Thanks."

"Anytime."

She blew out a breath. "Okay, let's go downstairs. You can give me my first cooking lesson."

Chapter Eleven

"I really appreciate the time, Savannah."

Savannah stretched out her long legs and glanced at the tape recorder Rebecca had set on the table between them. "It's no problem. I've got the time."

Rebecca scanned the living area of the cabin. It was bright and cluttered. Layla sat on the rug nearby and made engine noises as she raced a large plastic truck. "A woman with an active son and two kids in diapers can't have much time to spare."

"It only gets crazy around here ten or twelve times a day." Savannah slid a glance toward her daughter. "This seems to be a lull."

"How do you manage?" Rebecca blurted out. "I mean, three children—a new baby, your work, your home, your life."

"The first trick is to enjoy it. And I do. Since they're not here to get cocky about it, I'll tell you that my men do their share."

"You have a beautiful family." Hearing the wistfulness in her own voice, Rebecca shook it off. "Let me explain what I'm after. The book I'm working on deals with Antietam specifically, the battle, of course, but the angles I'm most interested in are the legends that surround this area, and personal experiences."

"Ghost stories."

"To some extent. The MacKade connection," Rebecca continued. "Regan and Rafe. They were both drawn to the inn, shared extraordinary experiences. Rafe came back to town for the inn, and Regan was drawn to it through him. The inn also played a major part in Cassie and Devin's lives and their relationship. I've interviewed each of them separately, and each corroborates the other's feelings and experiences. Some of those experiences were shared, some separate, but all seem to touch on the story of the two corporals."

"And you want me to tell you mine."

"Yes. I interviewed Jared this morning in his office. Oh, and I wanted to tell you I loved your paintings. Especially the one of the woods."

"Thanks. It was—is—the woods for us. If you want to use the word *connection*, I suppose that's ours." Savannah narrowed her eyes as she thought back. "The inn has a very strong pull. What Regan and Rafe have done there, and with Cassie and Devin living there, it's, I don't know, funneled off a great deal of the sadness. It was a sad place for a long time. But Regan tells me you tracked down some information on the Confederate corporal."

"Franklin Gray, yes."

"You said that Abigail had him identified and sent home to his family." Thinking of it, Savannah nodded. "That was very brave of her. And very kind."

"Abigail had children of her own. She must have imagined what that boy's mother would have felt. The never knowing. The Yankee boy's family would never have known. The other corporal..." Rebecca sighed, with just a hint of frustration. "That's all I've ever been able to pin down on him so far—he fought for the Union and was a corporal. At least that's the information that's been passed down through the MacKades."

"What the MacKades did for that wounded boy was brave and kind, too," Savannah commented. "But you need to find him, don't you? To learn his name, see his grave. To settle it."

"I suppose I do. They were killed so long ago, yet it seems... unfinished. They fought and died at each other's hands, two ordinary young men who never really lived. But their deaths affected so many other people. And it seems they still do. Isn't that part of what you feel in the woods, Savannah?"

Savannah tilted her head. "What do you consider the strongest emotions, Rebecca?"

"Love and hate. Everything else stems from that."

"Yeah." Pleased, Savannah smiled. "That's good, for an egghead. Anyway, that's what I felt in the woods. Love, I suppose that was for Jared, and for home. Hate—it was more the fear and violence that hatred leaves behind. Why were we both drawn there, and drawn most strongly to the spot where those two young boys fought more than a century ago? Connections?'' She lifted her shoulders. ''A need to set-tle it, or soften it, or understand it.''

''And did you?''

Savannah lifted a brow. ''Did Jared tell you that the first time we made love was in those woods?''

''No. No, he didn't.''

''He probably thought it would embarrass you.'' A slow, warm smile, utterly female, curved Savannah's lips. ''The cabin was empty, there was a perfectly good bed upstairs, but we went to the woods. Because it was right for us, because we were...con-nected. Because love heals.''

Rebecca thought of Shane and his tender gift to her. ''Yes, it does.''

''I've sat there and I've heard the rustle of leaves under boots, heard the shuddering breaths of fright-ened boys, the war cries, the crash of bayonets. I heard them before I'd heard the story.''

Rebecca's eyes narrowed with new interest. ''You didn't know about the two corporals when you came here?''

''No. Jared told me about it later, but I already knew. No, felt it.''

''Do you consider yourself psychic?''

Now Savannah chuckled. ''No more than any-one.'' A fretful wail had her glancing toward the stairs. ''Feeding time,'' she murmured. ''Be right back.''

''Baby,'' Layla said as her mother headed up-stairs. Toddling over, she handed Rebecca a doll. ''Baby.''

''Pretty baby.'' Understanding, Rebecca kissed the doll, then the child. ''Almost as pretty as you.''

With a grin that had the MacKade dimple winking, Layla squeezed the doll fiercely, then passed it back. "Mama." She danced in place, then squealed with delight when Savannah came down with Miranda fussing in her arms. "Baby! My baby!"

"Come and see," Savannah invited, settling down. Her free hand brushed over Layla's dark hair as the child bent over the infant.

"Baby, baby, baby," she cooed, placing wet kisses over Miranda's red, furious face.

"The baby's hungry," Savannah explained, and rolled her eyes at Rebecca. "And boy, does she let you know it!"

Rebecca watched as Savannah chattered with both of her daughters, fingers expertly unfastening buttons. The baby rooted, one tiny hand kneading a breast while her busy mouth found the nipple.

The envy, pure and primal, that swarmed through Rebecca shocked her. Because of it, she swallowed the questions that sprang to her mind. How does it feel to feed your child from your own body? Is it the intimacy of it that makes your eyes go soft?

"Would you rather finish this later?"

"No, this is fine."

"Regan looks like a Madonna when she nurses," Rebecca murmured. "You don't." Savannah's lifted brow had her laughing a little. "That's not an insult. I bought these tarot cards—part of my research. The Empress is a card of fertility, female power. That's what you look like."

"I can live with that."

"Well." Taking a deep breath, Rebecca got back to work. She asked her questions, moving Savannah from generalities to specifics, then moving her on to more esoteric matters. By the time she was finished, the baby was sleeping again, her mouth milky and slack.

"I'd like to ask a question now." Savannah rose to tuck Miranda into a cradle beside her chair.

"Sure."

"What exactly do you intend to do with all this? A book, I know, but I don't quite understand how you'll handle what I've told you. What we've all told you."

"I want to focus on the experiences of you three couples. And the influence of the legends on your lives. It's intriguing, and it's romantic, the way the past overlapped your present, and your future. Six people who've become three families," she explained, hands gesturing to illustrate. "Three families who are essentially one family. All of your relationships were affected by what happened here long before any of you were born. So, how much does the past influence us? How much does the power of place, the strength of who and what was, play on those open to accept it?"

"And you'll add your data to that, your evidence and your theories."

"That's right."

"And your reputation?" Savannah turned back. "What are all those institutes and the suits who run them going to say about Dr. Knight's interest in the occult?"

"Some will shake their heads and think it's too bad a brilliant young scientist lost her mind. Others...well, there are some excellent and serious studies being done on the paranormal at some of those institutes. And—" she smiled "—since I'm doing this for me, I don't really care what they think."

Savannah sat again, gathered Layla up in her arms. "Why haven't you talked to Shane?"

"Excuse me?"

"You said you'd interviewed all of us, and intend to use all of us in this book. But you never mentioned Shane."

"He's not comfortable with it." Rebecca busied herself tucking her tape recorder back into her bag. "He's been very tolerant of what I'm doing, but he doesn't like it. In any case, he doesn't fit into the equation. Six people, three couples. The connection."

Nodding, Savannah ran her tongue around her teeth. "You know, math isn't my strong point, but I figure eight people, four couples." She gave Layla a pat as the child wiggled down from her lap and went off to look for other entertainment. "What about your connection? You, Shane, the farm."

"It doesn't really apply."

"Of course it does. It's obvious you're in love with him."

"Is it?" Rebecca managed to say, relatively calmly. "You're mistaking attraction, affection and a physical relationship for— Hell. Are you sure you're not psychic?"

Poor thing, Savannah mused, sympathizing with any woman who'd tumbled for a MacKade. Poor, lucky thing. "You're a fairly controlled sort of woman, Rebecca. You don't advertise your feelings on your face. But I see things." Savannah waved a hand. "I'm an artist, and I have shamans for ancestors. You can chalk it up to that, or to the fact that one woman in love often recognizes another.''

Rebecca looked down at her hands. ''I don't know whether to be relieved or worried with that rundown.''

''I like you. I don't like everyone. I'm selective. Actually, I didn't think I'd like you at all.'' Comfortable, she stretched out her legs again. ''A professional intellectual, scientist, all those initials after your name. I got my high school equivalency when I was carrying Layla, and when Regan talked of you, all I saw was this enormous brain wearing horn-rim glasses.''

The image had Rebecca snorting out a laugh. She'd come a good ways, she thought, when such a description brought amusement rather than pain. ''If you sketch me that way, I'll hang it in my apartment.''

''That's a deal. Anyway, I did like you. Do like you. If I'd sat down and tried to piece together the woman who would suit Shane, she wouldn't have been anything like you. And I'd have been wrong. The farmer and the savant.'' The phrase made Savannah grin. Poor Shane, she thought. Poor, lucky Shane. ''In this case, it works. What are you going to do about it?''

''Enjoy it. While it lasts.''

''And that's enough?''

''It's more than I've had before.'' There would be a price, of course, she thought. She was willing to pay it. ''I'm a practical woman, Savannah.''

''Maybe. But how brave are you, and how dedicated? Are you really going to write a book, take all that time, put in all that effort, and leave out a piece of it? Your piece, and Shane's? Can you ignore that connection?''

Could she? Rebecca asked herself as she walked back to the farm through the woods. For the book, yes. She could and would do that for Shane. Personally, she'd accepted that the connection between them would remain with her forever.

Yet she could leave, would leave. It would hurt, but she would survive it. Intellectually, she knew no one really died of a broken heart. Emotionally, she suspected some could.

But it would be easier to live when she'd had love than it had been to exist without ever knowing it.

She knew her Greek tragedies well. There was always pleasure, and there was always payment.

Her bill, so to speak, was coming due, she knew. If Savannah could read her heart so easily, others would. Shane might, and then the payment could become too high to bear.

He meant too much to her for her to put him in an awkward position. She would have to start considering that first step away.

Tomorrow was the anniversary of the battle. She felt it important, even imperative, that she stay on the farm through the day, and perhaps the next. Then it would probably be best if she moved back to Regan's. A few days, a short transitory period before she went back to New York.

She stepped through the trees and looked at the farm. There was smoke coming out of the chimney from the living room fireplace. It was just chilly enough to warrant one. She could see the house itself, strong stone, painted wood, the silos and sheds and buildings.

It would, she realized, be almost as wrenching to leave the place as it would be to leave Shane. She'd been happier here than she'd ever been in her life. She'd found love here.

So she would be grateful, rather than regretful.

Walk away, a voice nagged in her brain, *rather than risk.*

Suddenly chilled, she rubbed her arms and began to cross the fallow field.

She saw the car zip up the curve of the lane and park at the side of the house. A quick, friendly toot of the horn, and the dogs were scrambling to greet the redhead who climbed out.

The air was clear enough to carry the woman's laugh to where Rebecca stopped. And the distance wasn't so great that she couldn't see Shane's lightning grin as he came around the side of the house to meet the woman.

Jealousy ebbed and flowed, ebbed and flowed, in a nasty, unpredictable tide as Rebecca watched them embrace easily. As the woman's arms stayed linked around Shane's neck.

Oh, no, you don't, she warned silently. He's still mine. He's mine until I walk away.

They stayed close together as they spoke, and there was more laughter, another quick kiss, before the woman stepped away and got back into her car.

Shane ruffled both dogs, straightened, waved. Rebecca knew the moment he spotted her in the field, and began to walk toward the house again. The car darted down the lane between them, then disappeared around the curve.

"Hey." He tucked his thumbs in his front pockets. "How's Savannah?"

"Fine. I had a chance to look at some of her paintings. They're wonderful."

"Yeah." With his instincts warning him to proceed with caution, Shane tried to read Rebecca's face. "Ah, that was Frannie Spader. You met Frannie."

"I thought I recognized her." Because they wanted attention, and because it was a good ploy, Rebecca bent to pet the dogs.

"She just dropped by."

"So I saw. I want to transcribe this interview."

"Rebecca." He touched her arm to stop her. "There's nothing going on here. She's a friend. She stopped by."

It was pure self-defense that had her arching a brow. "Why do you feel you have to clarify that?"

"Because I— Look, Fran and I used to be... We used to be," he finished, furious with himself. "Now we're not, and haven't been since... well, since you came to town. We're friends."

Oh, it was satisfying to watch him squirm. "Do you think I require an explanation?"

"No. Yes." Damn it. He imagined himself strolling along and coming across Rebecca hugging another man. Someone would have to die. "I don't want you to get the wrong idea, that's all."

"Do you think I have the wrong idea?"

"Will you cut that out?" he demanded, and paced away, then back again. "I hate when you do that. I really hate it."

"When I do what?"

"Make everything a question. How do you feel, what do you think?" He whirled back to her, eyes shooting sparks of temper. "Damn it, if you had a question, it should have been 'What in the hell were you doing kissing another woman?'"

"Do you feel a show of jealousy would be appropriate?" When he only scowled at her, she shrugged. "I'm sorry I can't accommodate you. Clearly, you had a life before I came here, and you'll have one after I'm gone."

"That's it. Throw the past in my face."

"Is that what you think I'm doing?"

He snarled. "Can't you fight like a regular person?"

"When there's something to fight about. Your friends are your business. And as I have no idea how many of those . . . friends I might run into every time I go into town, it would be remarkably unproductive of me to worry about it."

His brain was screaming out for him to let it go, but his mouth just refused to obey. "Look, Rebecca, if I'd slept with as many women as some people think, I'd never have gotten out of bed. And I haven't had sex with every woman I've gone out with, either. I don't— Why the hell am I telling you this?"

"That was going to be my next question. And, in my opinion, what you're doing is projecting—your feelings, your anticipated reaction to a situation, onto me. Added to that is a sense of guilt, and annoyance resulting from that guilt. In transferring the annoyance from yourself to me, you—"

"Shut up." His eyes as volatile as a storm at sea, he grabbed her face in his hands. "She came by to see if I wanted to go out later. I told her no. She asked if I was involved with you. I told her yes, very involved.

We talked for another minute, she said she'd see me around. That's it. Satisfied?''

Her heart was tripping lightly, quickly, in her chest. But her voice was cool, and faintly curious. "Did I give you the impression that I was dissatisfied?''

His eyes narrowed, flashed. Rebecca found it very satisfying. Almost as satisfying as his frustrated oath as he turned on his heel and stalked away.

Nice job, Dr. Knight, she told herself. She didn't think Shane was going to be kissing anyone else for a while. Humming to herself, she strolled into the house.

She really did have work to do, she thought, and patted one of her video monitors as she passed. But she could take just a moment to savor the sense of smugness.

The poor guy had been so predictable. Classic re-actions. Alarm at the thought that something, how-ever innocent, could be interpreted badly. The added weight of his infamous career as a ladies' man. Not a womanizer, she mused. One day she might explain to him the difference between a man who loved and ap-preciated woman and one who used them.

And then, she thought, snickering on her way to the kitchen, his sense of unease, then irritation at her reasonable reaction. Direct hit on the ego.

It was so much more interesting to study the games men and women played with each other when you were in the middle of the field than when you were observing from the stands.

She might just do a paper on it, she mused, going to the window. Once she'd carved out enough emo-tional distance. By then she would know not only what it was like to fall in love, to be in love, but what it felt like to lose at love.

One day she might find the courage to ask him what she had meant to him, what the time they had spent together had meant to him in the scheme of things. Yeah, she thought, amused at herself. She might find the courage for that in a decade or two.

Telling herself it was now that mattered, and wondering if the little incident would garner her more flowers, she decided to try her hand at cooking dinner solo.

It was really all just formulas, after all. And she had Regan's formula—no, recipe, she reminded herself—for fried chicken in her bag. Digging it out, she read it through once and committed it to memory. Since Shane's kitchen didn't run to aprons, she tucked a dishcloth in the waistband of her slacks, and got down to some serious experimenting.

It was actually soothing, she discovered as she coated chicken with herbed flour. At least on a casual level. She imagined that if anyone had to plan and cook and deal with the time and mess every day, day after day, meal after meal, it would be tedious.

But, as a hobby, it had its points. If she could just keep this particular hobby from becoming a vocation, as so many of her others had, she'd be just fine.

When she had chicken frying in hot oil in a cast-iron skillet, she stepped back and congratulated herself. It smelled good, it sounded good, it looked good. Therefore, according to basic laws, it should taste good.

Wouldn't Shane be surprised, and perhaps even more baffled, when he came in and found dinner cooking?

It was milking time, she thought, poking at the crisping chicken with a kitchen fork. And night was coming earlier, as the days shortened toward the still-distant winter....

Would she see the camp fires burning if she looked out the window? The soldiers were so close, close and waiting for dawn and the battle.

She wished John would come in. Once he was in and the animals were settled, they could shut up the house. They would be safe here. They had to be safe here. She couldn't lose another child. Couldn't live through it. Nor could John. She pressed a hand over the one covering her womb, as if to protect it from any threat, any harm. She desperately hoped it would be a son. Not to replace the one they'd lost. Johnnie could never be replaced, never be forgotten. But if the babe she carried was a son, it would somewhat ease the worst of John's grief.

He suffered. He suffered so, and there was no comfort for it. She could love him, tend him, share the grief, but she couldn't end it. The girls tried, and God knew they were a joy. But Johnnie was gone. Every day the war went on was another painful reminder of that loss.

Maybe it would end here. She turned the chicken in the pan, as she'd done so often in her life. Would that be some sort of justice, for this horrible war to end here, where her son had been born?

Was the man who had killed her son out there, right now, sitting, waiting, in the Union camp? Who would he kill tomorrow? Or would it be his blood that would seep into the land she had walked over for so many years?

Why wouldn't they go away? Just go away and leave the living in peace with their sorrows....

Hot grease popped out of the pan and seared the side of Rebecca's hand. She barely felt it as she staggered backward. Emotions, thoughts, words, sounds, reeled in her head.

Possession, she thought, dimly. This was possession. And, for the first time in her life, she fainted.

Primed to fight, Shane burst through the door. "And another thing—" he began, before he saw Rebecca crumpled on the kitchen floor, before his heart stopped.

He streaked forward, dropped down beside her to drag her into her arms. "Rebecca." His hands were running over her face, chafing her wrists. "Rebecca, come on now. Snap out of it." Terrified into clumsiness, he rocked her, kissed her, begged her. Until her eyes fluttered open.

"Shane."

"That's right." Relief poured through him in a flood. "Just lie still, baby, till you feel better."

"I was her," she murmured, fighting off the fog. "I was her for a minute. I have to check my equipment."

"The hell with your equipment." It was pitifully easy to hold her in place. "Do as you're told and lie still. Did you hit your head? Are you hurt anywhere?"

"I don't . . . I don't think so. What happened?"

"You tell me. I walked in and you were on the floor."

"Good Lord." She took a deep, steadying breath and let her head rest in the crook of his arm. "I fainted. Imagine that."

"I don't have to imagine it. You just scared ten years off my life." Now, naturally, there was fury to coat over the fear. "What the hell are you doing fainting? Did you eat today? Damn it, you never eat enough to keep a bird alive. You don't get enough sleep, either. Down four or five hours, then you're up prowling around, or clacking away at that stupid computer."

He was working himself up into a rare state, but he couldn't stop. "Well, that's going to change. You're going to start taking care of yourself. You're nothing but bones and nerve. Didn't they teach you anything about basic bodily needs in those fancy schools? Or don't you think they apply to you?"

She let him run on until her head stopped spinning. He was ranting about taking her to the doctor, checking her into the hospital, getting vitamins. Finally, she held up a hand and put it over his mouth.

"I've never fainted before in my life, and since I didn't care for it, I don't intend to make it a habit. Now, if you'll calm down a minute and let me up, the chicken's burning."

He said something incredible and unlikely when applied to burning chicken, but he did haul her into a chair. Moving quickly, he flicked off the heat. "What the hell were you doing?"

"I was cooking. I think it was going to be fairly successful, too. Maybe it can be salvaged."

He grunted, turned to the tap and ran a glass of water for her. "Drink."

She started to tell him he needed it more than she, then decided against it. Obediently she sipped water. "I was cooking," she said again, "and letting my mind wander. Then the thoughts weren't mine any longer. They were very clear—very personal, you could say. But they weren't mine. They were Sarah's."

Ice skidded up his spine. "You're just letting yourself get too wrapped up in all this stuff."

"Shane, I'm a sensible woman. A rational one. I know what happened here. She was cooking chicken." With a shake of her head, Rebecca set the glass on the table. "Isn't it odd that I would have decided to try Regan's recipe tonight, September 16? Sarah was cooking chicken the night before the battle."

"So now you know what they ate."

"Yes," she said, facing down his sarcasm. "Now I know. She was frying it, worried about her family, thinking of her son and the baby she carried. Wondering who would die in the morning. Soldiers were camped not far from here, waiting for dawn. She was frying chicken, and her husband was out with the animals. She wanted him to come in, to come inside so that they could close it all out and just be together. She worried about him. She'd have done anything to ease his mind."

"I think you're working too hard," Shane said carefully. "And I think you've let the fact that the anniversary is tomorrow influence you."

Steady again, she rose. "You know that's not true. You know what's here and you've decided not to face it. That's your choice, and I respect that. Even though I know some nights you dream, and the dreams trouble you, I respect your decision and your privacy. I expect you to show my work and my needs the same respect.''

"My dreams are my business."

"I've just said so. I'm not asking you to tell me anything."

"No, you never ask, Rebecca." He jammed his hands into his pockets. "You just wait and whittle a person down with waiting. I don't want any part of this."

"Do you want me to go?"

When he didn't answer, she braced herself, spoke calmly. "I suppose I'll have to ask. It's important to me to be here in the morning. I can't give you clear, rational data on why, only my feelings. I'd appreciate it very much if you'd let me stay, at least another day."

"No one's asked you to go, have they?" He snapped the words out, furious with himself now. Why should he panic at the thought of her packing up? There had never been any promises. He didn't make them, didn't want them. "You want to stay, stay—but leave me out of it. I've got some work to finish up, then I'm going out."

"All right."

He wanted desperately for her to ask him where, and would have snapped her head off if she questioned him. Of course, she didn't, so he couldn't. All he could do was walk out, when all he wanted to do was stay.

Chapter Twelve

He thought about getting drunk. It wasn't a problem-solver, but it did have its points. It was a shame he wasn't in the mood for it. Arguing with someone was a better idea, and since Rebecca wasn't going to accommodate him, he headed for town, and Devin.

He'd always been able to count on Devin for a good fight.

Shane figured it was a bonus when he found not only Devin in the sheriff's office, but Rafe, too.

"Hey, we were just talking about getting together a poker game." Rafe greeted him with a slap on the shoulder. "Got any money?"

"Got a beer around here?"

"This is a place of law and order," Devin said solemnly, then jerked his head toward the back room. "Couple in the cooler. You up for a game?"

"Maybe." Shane stalked into the back room. "I can do what I want when I want, can't I? I don't have to check with a woman, like you guys do."

Devin and Rafe exchanged looks. "I'll give Jared a call," Rafe said, picking up the phone as Shane came back in guzzling beer.

While Rafe dialed the phone and murmured into it, Devin propped his feet on his desk. "So, what's Rebecca up to?"

"She doesn't have to check with me, either."

"Ah, had a little spat, did you?" Enjoying the idea, Devin crossed his arms behind his head. "She kick you out?"

"It's my damn house," Shane shot back. "And Reasonable Rebecca doesn't spat. She changes," he went on, gesturing with the beer. "Right in front of your eyes. One minute she's tough and smart and cocky. The next she's soft and lost and so sweet you'd kill anybody who'd try to hurt her. Then she's cool— Oh, she's so cool, and controlled, and—" He gulped down beer. "Analytical. How the hell are you supposed to keep up?"

"Well," Devin mused, "you can't call her boring."

"Anything but. She thinks she is, at least some of the time. Hell, I don't know what she thinks she is." Shane brooded into the bottle. "Just today, she comes across Frannie kissing me. Does she get mad, does she start a fight, accuse me of anything? No. Not that it wasn't perfectly innocent, but the point is that if you're sleeping with somebody you shouldn't like the idea of them kissing somebody else. Right?"

Rafe had hung up the phone and was watching his brother carefully. "I'd agree with that. You agree with that, Dev?"

"Pretty much, yeah."

Pleased with the unity of spirit, Shane lifted the bottle again. "There you go. But Dr. Knight, she's as cool as you please. Studying me like I'm a smear on a lab slide again. I hate when she does that."

"Who wouldn't?" Rafe said, and sat down to enjoy himself.

Soothed by brotherly understanding, Shane finished off the first beer, then popped open the second. "And another thing—how come she doesn't ask where all this is leading? Tell me that. Women are always asking where all this is leading. That's how you keep things from getting too intense, by setting down the cards, you know."

"Is that how?" Devin smiled serenely.

"Sure. But she doesn't ask." He chugged down beer. That was why things had gotten so intense. He needed to believe that. "And you'd think she'd get in the way, wouldn't you? You'd think she'd get in the damn way, living there, but she just sort of fits."

"Does she?" Devin grinned and winked at Rafe.

"Sort of. I mean, there she is at breakfast in the morning, and she's always got something to talk about. She works in the kitchen most of the time, but she never gets in the way, and you start expecting her to be there."

Rafe looked around as the door opened and Jared walked in with a large brown bag. Jared set it on Devin's desk and took out a six-pack. "We playing here?"

"Maybe later." To keep the interruption at a minimum, Devin gestured Jared to a chair. "Shane's on a roll."

"Yeah." Jared looked at Shane. "What's he rolling about?"

"Rebecca. You were saying?"

"The bedroom smells like her," Shane muttered. "She doesn't leave any of her stuff laying around, and it still smells like her. Soap, and that stuff she rubs on her skin."

"Uh-oh," Jared said, and helped himself to a beer.

"You know, her parents sent her to boarding school when she was six. Practically a baby. She never had a chance to be a kid. Sometimes when she laughs, she looks a little surprised by the sound of it." He paused, thought about it. "She's got a great laugh."

Jared turned to Rafe. "She kick him out?"

"He says not."

"It's my damn house," Shane reminded them all. "My house, my land. I'm the one who says what goes on around there. If I don't like that stupid, idiotic ridiculous equipment of hers, then that's it. I do like that she's wrapped herself up in all this bull, she's wearing herself down. I'm not coming in finding her in a heap on the floor again."

"What?" Amusement fled as Devin straight in his chair. "What happened?"

"She fainted—far as I can tell. She says she encounter with our great-grandmother." He d beer to wash both worry and unease out of tem. "Yeah, right. They're both frying chic night before the battle. I'm not getting inv that."

"Is she all right?" Rafe asked.

"Would I be here if she wasn't?" He raked his fingers through his hair and fought to block out the image of her pale, small, still form on the kitchen floor. But he couldn't. "She scared the hell out of me, damn it. Damn it." He squeezed his eyes shut for a moment, rubbed the heel of his hand over his aching heart. "I can't take her being hurt. I can't stand it. The woman's ripping at me."

With an effort, he pulled himself back, took another gulp from the bottle. "She bounces back," he muttered. "I've never seen anybody bounce back like she does. She's fine now, dandy, back in control. She's not pushing me into getting hooked up with that business. She's not going to hook me into anything."

"Brother." With some sympathy, Jared opened another beer and passed it to Shane. "You're already hooked."

"Like hell."

"At a guess, how many times do you think about her in a given day?"

"I don't know." Annoyed, Shane decided getting drunk wasn't such a bad idea after all. "I don't count."

In lawyer mode now, Jared briskly cross-examined he witness. "Anyone else you've thought about that uch, that often?"

'So what? She's living with me. You think about ebody who's in the same house day and night."

fe studied his nails. "It's just sex."

ch e hell it is." Like a bullet, Shane was out of his ists ready. "She's not just a warm body." He caught himself, and his brother's sly grin. "I'm not an animal."

"That's a switch." Unconcerned, Rafe sampled his own beer. "How many other women have you wanted since Rebecca came along?"

Zip. Zero. Zilch. Terror. "That's not the point. The point is..." He sat again, brooded into his beer. "I forgot."

"The point is," Devin said, picking up the threads, "you've lost your balance and you're falling fast."

"He's already hit," Jared put in. "He just doesn't have the sense to know it. But, being a sensible woman, Rebecca might not fall so easy, especially for you."

"What the hell's wrong with me?"

"As I was saying," Jared continued. "She's got a life in New York, a career, interests. You might have a problem keeping her from wriggling away. You'll have to be pretty slick to convince her to marry you."

Shane choked, coughed, and gulped more beer. "You're crazy. I'm not marrying anybody."

Rafe only smiled. "Wanna bet?"

Because Shane was terribly pale, Devin took pity on him. "Have another beer, pal. You can bunk in the back room and sleep it off."

It seemed like an excellent suggestion.

She didn't sleep. It wasn't only because Shane wasn't there and the house seemed to come alive around her. It was the wait for morning, through the longest night of her life.

She worked. It had always helped her through crises, small and large. She packed. The systematic removal of her clothing, the neat folding of it into suitcases, was a sign that she was ready to go on with the rest of her life.

If she had a worry, it was that she and Shane would part on uneasy terms. That she didn't want. When he came back, she told herself, she would try to put things back into perspective and achieve some kind of balance.

But he didn't come back, and the hours passed slowly to dawn.

When the sun had just begun to rise, and the gray mist hung over the land, swallowing the barn, she stepped outside.

It was impossible for her to believe, at that moment, that anyone wouldn't feel what she felt. The fear, the anticipation, the rage and the sorrow.

It took so little imagination for her to see the infantry marching through that soft curtain of fog, bodies and bayonets tearing it so that it swirled back and reformed. The muffled sound of boots on earth, the dull glint of brass and steel.

That first burst from the cannons, those first cries.

Then there would be hell.

"What are you doing out here?"

Rebecca jolted, stared. It was Shane, stepping through that river of mist. He looked pale, gritty-eyed, and angry enough that she resisted the need to rush forward and hold him.

"I didn't hear you come home."

"Just got here." She hadn't slept. He could see the fatigue in her eyes, the shadows under them, and detested the stab of guilt. "You're shivering. You're barefoot, for God's sake. Go back inside. Go to bed."

"You look tired," she said, knowing her voice was more brittle than cool.

"I'm hung over," he said flatly. "Some of us humans get that way when we drink too much. Aren't you going to ask me where I've been, who I've been with?"

She lifted a hand, rubbed it gently over her heart. It still beat, she thought vaguely, even when it was shattered. "Are you trying to hurt me?"

"Maybe I am. Maybe I'm trying to see if I can."

She nodded and turned back toward the house. "You can."

"Rebecca—" But she was already closing the door behind her, leaving him feeling like something slimy that had crawled from under a rock. Cursing her, he headed toward the milking parlor.

They stayed out of each other's way through the morning. Rather than work in the kitchen, she closed herself in the guest room and focused fiercely on the job at hand. So they would part at odds, she thought. Perhaps that was best. It might be easier, in the long run, to hide behind resentment and anger.

From the window in her room, she saw him. He didn't seem to be working. Marking time, she decided, until she cleared out. Well, he would have to wait a little longer. She wasn't leaving until the day was over.

"Where are you, Sarah?" she murmured, pacing the room, which was beginning to feel like a cell. "You wanted me here. I know you wanted me here. For what?"

As she passed the window, she looked out again. He was walking across the yard now, past the kitchen garden, where he had late tomatoes, greens, squash. He stopped, checked something. For ripeness, she supposed.

It was painful to look at him. Yet too painful to contemplate looking away. Had she really believed she could take the experience of love and loss as some sort of adventure—or, worse, as an experiment on the human condition? That she could examine it, analyze, perhaps write about it?

No, she would never, never get over him.

When he straightened from the little garden and walked toward one of the stone outbuildings, she turned away. No, she wouldn't wait until the end of the day after all. That was too cruel. She would speak to him again, one last time, and then she would go.

She'd send for the equipment, she told herself as she went downstairs. She would make her exit with dignity, albeit with dispatch. To Regan's, she told herself, breathing carefully. To run back to New York just now would look cowardly. It was pointless to make him feel bad, to let him know he'd had her heart and broken it.

Let him think that it had simply been an experience, one that was over now, one they could both remember fondly.

She was never coming back. At the base of the stairs, she stopped to press her hand to her mouth. Never coming back to this town, this battleground, this house. Though she would be in full retreat, she would not run.

She never glanced at the monitors, the gauges. Down the hall, she trailed her fingers over wood and paint, as if to absorb the texture into memory.

At the kitchen doorway, the power punched like a fist. . . .

Stew cooking. The distant pop of gunfire. . .

Weak, she leaned against the wall as the door opened.

She knew it was Shane. The rational part of her mind recognized the shape of him, the stance, even the smell. But with some inner eye she saw a man carrying a bleeding boy. . . .

My God, my God, John. Is he dead?

Not yet.

Put him on the table. I need towels. Oh, so much blood. Hurry. He's so young. He's just a boy.

Like Johnnie.

So like Johnnie. Young, bleeding, dying. The uniform was filthy and wet with blood. The new stripe of his rank was still bright on the shoulder of the tattered jacket. There was a rustle of worn paper from a letter in the inside pocket as she peeled the uniform away to see the horror of his wounds.

Just a boy. Too many dying boys. . .

Rebecca saw it, could see the scene in the kitchen perfectly. The blood, the boy, those who tried to help him. There, the letter in Sarah's hands, the paper worn where it had been creased and recreased, read and reread. The words seemed to leap out at her. . . .

Dear Cameron . . .

"They couldn't save him," Shane said carefully. "They tried."

"Yes." After the breath she'd been holding was expelled, Rebecca pressed her lips together. "They tried so hard."

"At first, he only saw the uniform. The enemy. He was glad that a Yankee had died there. Then he saw the face, and he saw his son in it. So he brought him home. It was all he could do."

"It was the right thing to do, the human thing."

"They wanted that boy to live, Rebecca."

"I know." Her breath shuddered out, shuddered in. "They fought as hard as they could. All the rest of that day, through the night, sitting with him. Praying. Listening to him, when he could speak. Shane, there was too much love in this house for them not to try, not to fight for that one young boy's life."

"But they lost him." Eyes grim, Shane stepped forward. "And it was like losing their son again."

"He didn't die alone, or forgotten."

"But they buried him in an unmarked grave."

"She was afraid." Tears trembled out, rolling down Rebecca's cheeks. "She was afraid for her husband, for her family. Nothing meant more to her. If anyone found out that boy had died here, and John a Rebel sympathizer who'd lost a son to the Yankees, they might have taken John from her. She couldn't have stood it. She begged him not to tell, to dig the grave at night so no one would ever know. Oh, she grieved for that boy, for the mother who would never know where or when or how he died. She read the letter."

"Yeah, then they buried the letter from his mother with him."

"There was no envelope, Shane. No address. Nothing to tell them where he had come from, or who was waiting for him to come home. Just the two pages, the writing close and crowded as if she'd wanted to jam every thought, every feeling into them." A breath shuddered out. "I saw it. I could read it, just as Sarah did . . . Dear Cameron."

Shane's eyes went dark, his stomach muscles tightened, twisted. "That's my middle name. Cameron was my grandfather's name. Cameron James Mac-Kade, John and Sarah's second son. He was born six months after the Battle of Antietam." Shane took a steadying breath. "The name's come down through the MacKades ever since. Every generation has a Cameron."

"They named their child after the boy they couldn't save." Helplessly Rebecca rubbed the tears from her cheeks with the flats of her hands. "They didn't forget him, Shane. They did everything they could."

"And then they buried him in an unmarked grave."

"Don't hate her for it. She loved her husband, and was afraid for him."

"I don't hate her for it." Suddenly weary, Shane scrubbed his hands over his face. "But it's my life now, Rebecca, my land. I can't change what happened, and I'm sick of being haunted by it."

She offered a hand. "Do you know where he's buried?"

"No, I've always shut that part out." As he'd tried, most of his life, to shut it all out. All those wavering memories, those misty dreams. "I never wanted any part of this."

"Why did you come in now, tell me now?"

"I don't know, exactly." Resigned, he dropped his hands. "I saw him, beside the smokehouse. Bleeding, asking me to help him." He drew a long breath. "It's not the first time. I couldn't not come in, not tell you anymore. You're part of it. You knew that all along."

"He's buried in the meadow," she murmured. "Wildflowers grow there." She reached for his hand again, tightened her fingers on his. "Come with me."

They walked out toward the meadow, through the bright wash of sun. The mountains were alive with color, and the flowers underfoot were going to seed. There was the smell of grass and growing things. When she stopped, the tears still fell quietly.

For a moment, she could say nothing, could only stare down at the ground where she had once dropped her first clutch of wildflowers.

"They did their best for him. Not far from here, another man killed a boy simply because of the color of his uniform. These people tried to save one, despite it." She leaned into Shane when he circled her shoulders with his arm. "They cared."

"Yeah, they cared. They still can't leave him here alone."

"We make parks out of our battlefields to remember," she said quietly. "It's important to remember. He needs a marker, Shane. They would have given him one, if they could have."

Could it be as simple as that? he wondered. And as human? "All right." He stopped questioning and nodded. "We'll give him one. And maybe we'll all have some peace."

"There's more love than grief here," she murmured. "And it is yours, Shane—your home, your land, your heritage. Whatever lives on through it, through you is admirable. You should be very proud of what you have, and what you are."

"I always felt as though they were pushing at me. I resented it." Yet it had eased now, standing there with her in the sun, on his land. "I didn't see why I should be the one to be weighed down with their problems, their emotions." He looked over the fields, the hills, and felt most of his weariness pass. "Maybe I do now. It's always been more mine than any of my brothers'. More even than it was my father's, my mother's. We all loved it, we all worked it, but—"

"But you stayed, because you loved it more." She rose on her toes and kissed him gently. "And you understand it more. You're a good man, Shane. And a good farmer. I won't forget you."

Before he realized what she was doing, she'd turned away. "What are you talking about? Where are you going?"

"I thought you might like some time alone here." She smiled, brushing at the tears drying on her cheeks. "It seems a personal moment to me, and I really have to finish getting my things together."

"What things?"

"My things." She backed away as she spoke. "Now that we've settled this, I'm going to stay with Regan for a few days before I go back to New York. I haven't had as much time to visit with her as I'd planned."

She might as well have hit him over the head with a hammer. The quiet relief he'd begun to feel at facing what had haunted him was rudely, nastily swallowed up by total panic.

"You're leaving? Just like that? Experiment's over, see you around?"

"I'm only going to Regan's, for a few days. I've already stayed here longer than I originally intended, and I'm sure you'd like your house back. I'm very grateful for everything."

"You're grateful," he repeated. "For everything?"

"Yes, very." She was terrified her smile would waver. Quick, was all she could think, get away quick. "I'd like to stay in touch, if you don't mind. See how things are going with you."

"We can exchange cards at Christmas."

"I think we can do better." Through sheer grit, she kept that easy smile on her face. "Farm boy, it's been an experience."

Mouth slack with shock, he watched her walk away. She was dumping him. She'd just put him through the most emotional, most wrenching, most stunning experience of his life, and she was just walking away.

Well, fine, he thought, scowling at her retreating back. Dandy. That made it clean. He didn't want complications, or big, emotional parting scenes.

The hell he didn't.

She'd reached the kitchen door and just stepped over the threshold when he caught up with her. A tornado of temper, he snagged her shoulders, whirled her around.

"Just sex and science, is that it, Doc? I hope to hell I gave you plenty of data for one of your stinking papers."

"What are you—"

"Don't you want one last experiment for the road?"

He dragged her up hard against him, crushed his mouth down on hers. It was brutal, and it was fierce. For the first time, she was afraid of him, and what he was capable of.

"Shane." Shuddering, she wrenched her mouth free. "You're hurting me."

"Good." But he released her, jerking away so that she nearly stumbled. "You deserve it. You cold-blooded—" He managed to stop himself before he said something he wouldn't be able to live with later. "How can you have slept with me, have shared everything we've shared, and then just turn around and walk, like it meant nothing to you but a way to pass some time?"

"I thought—I thought that's how it was done. I've heard people say that you stay friends with all the women you've—"

"Don't throw my past up at me!" he shouted. "Damn it, nothing's been the same since you came here. You've tangled up my life long enough. I want you to go. I want you out."

"I'm going," she managed, and took one careful step, then another, until she'd reached the doorway.

"For God's sake, Rebecca, don't leave me."

She turned back, steadied herself with one hand against the jamb. "I don't understand you."

"You want me to beg." The humiliation was almost as vicious as the temper. "Fine, I'll beg. Please don't go. Don't walk out on me. I don't think I can live without you."

She put a hand to her head as she stared at him. All she could see was all that emotion swirling in his eyes. Too much emotion, impossible to decipher. "You want me to stay? But—"

"What's the big deal about New York?" he demanded. "So they've got museums and restaurants. You want to go to a restaurant, I'll take you to a damn restaurant. Now. Get your coat."

"I—I'm not hungry."

"Fine. You don't need a restaurant. See?" He sounded insane, he realized. Hell, he was insane. "You've got that fancy computer, the modem and all those gizmos. You can work anywhere. You can work here."

She wasn't used to having her brain frazzled. In defense, she latched on to the last thing he'd said. "You want me to work here?"

"What's wrong with that? You've been getting along here, haven't you?"

"Yes, but—"

"Leave your equipment set up everywhere." He threw up his hands. "I don't care." In a lightning move, he leaped forward and lifted her off her feet with hands under her elbows. "I don't care," he repeated. "I'm used to it. Set up a transmitter in the hay barn, put a satellite dish on the roof. Just don't leave."

The first hint of a smile curved her lips. Perhaps relationships weren't her forte, but she believed she was getting the idea. "You want me to stay here?"

"How many languages do you speak?" Sheer frustration had him shaking her. "Can't you understand English?" He dropped her back on her feet so that he could pace. "Didn't I just say that? I can't believe I'm saying it, but I am. I'm not losing you," he muttered. "I'm not losing what I have with you. I've never felt this way about anyone. I didn't want to, but you changed everything. Now you're in my head all the time, and the thought of you not being where I can see you or touch you rips my heart out. It rips my damn heart out!" he shouted, spinning toward her with blood in his eye. "You've got no right to do that to somebody, then leave!"

She started to speak, but the look on his face when she opened her mouth stopped her cold.

"I love you, Rebecca. Oh, God, I love you. And I have to sit down."

His knees were buckling. He was sure he'd crawl next. To get some control, he pressed the heels of his hands against his eyes. Whatever the humiliation, he would take it, as long as she stayed.

Then he looked up, looked at her. And she was weeping. His heart stopped thudding, split apart and sank.

"I'm sorry. I'm sorry. I've got no right to treat you this way, talk to you this way. Please don't cry."

She took a sobbing breath. "In my whole life, no one has ever said those words to me. Not once, in my whole life. You can't possibly know what it's like to hear them from you now."

He rose again, resenting everyone who had ever taken her for granted, including himself. "Don't tell me it's too late for me to say them. I'll make it up to you, Rebecca, if you let me."

"I was afraid to tell you how much I love you. I thought you wouldn't want me to."

He took a moment before he tried to speak, a moment to let what she'd said seep in and heal his dented heart. "I want you to. I need you to. You're not going."

She was shaking her head when he pulled her into his arms. "I'm not going anywhere."

"You're in love with me."

"Oh, yes."

"Thank God." He covered her mouth with his while joy fountained through him. "I've been falling for you since I picked you up at the airport. You were so snotty, I couldn't resist you." A thought intruded, made him wince. "Rebecca, last night—"

"It doesn't matter."

"Yes, it does. I was with my brothers, down at Devin's office. I got drunk and slept it off on the cot in the back room. I was angry about what was happening here, and what had happened inside me, for you. Stupid." He lowered his brow to hers. "I didn't know if you just let go a little, it could all be so right. You were always meant to come here. Do you believe that?"

"Yes." She cupped her hands on his cheeks. The full power of it struck her like light. "We're connected."

"That's one way to put it. I like 'I love you' better. I really like that. Who'd have thought?"

"I like it, too, better than anything." Blissful, she snuggled into his arms. "And I won't leave my equipment spread around the house. Since we're going to be living together, we need some sense of order."

"Living together." He tipped her face back, kissed her forehead, her nose, her lips. "Wrong. We've already been there, sort of. You're going to marry me."

"Marry." Her head spun. "You." Her legs turned to water. "I have to sit down now."

"No, you don't. I'll hold you up." That lightning MacKade grin flashed before he began to trace kisses over her face, move his hands up and down and over her. Damn, but she was cute when that brain of her clicked off. "Marry me, Rebecca," he murmured. "You might as well say yes. I'll just talk you into it."

Marriage. Family. Children. Shane. Why would he have to talk her into something she wanted more than anything in the world? "I can't think."

"Good." They'd keep it that way awhile, he decided, and nipped gently at her jaw. "I love you. Mmm...pretty Rebecca, I love you. Say, 'I love you, too.'"

The muscles in her thighs went lax. "I love you, too."

"Marry me, Rebecca." His curved lips skimmed over hers, down her chin and back again. "Be my wife, have my children, stay with me. Say yes. Say, 'Yes, I'll marry you, Shane.'"

"Yes." The strength came back into her arms as she threw them around his neck. "Yes, I'll marry you, Shane."

He nibbled around to her ear. "Say, 'I'll cook for you night and day, Shane.'"

"I'll—" Her eyes popped open. The most momentous event of her life ended in laughter. "Sneaky. Very sneaky, farm boy."

"It was worth a shot, Becky." Laughing with her, he gathered her into his arms and swept her in circles. "But I'll take the best two out of three."

Epilogue

Sunlight glinted off snow and the ice that crusted over it, so that the land sparkled clean and pure. They would all be there soon, Rebecca thought. All the MacKades, with their noise and their energy. And they would come here, to the meadow where a simple stone marker rose out of the untrampled snow and cast its thin gray shadow over white.

But she had come first. She and her husband. The word, even after three months of marriage, still made her heart trip with pure joy. Shane Cameron Mac-Kade was her husband. This day, the first day of the new year, she had love, she had a family, and the future was hers.

She slipped her hand in his, the hand that carried the simple gold band she'd wanted on her finger. And together they stood.

"It's what they all wanted," Shane said quietly. "Acknowledgment for a life that ended too soon. Acknowledgment is a kind of peace, don't you think?"

"That's what you feel here now, in the air. And I'll find his family's descendants." She turned her head, smiled up at Shane. "It'll take time—but we have time."

"I'll help you." He tipped her face up for a kiss. "We all will. It's a MacKade project. And you've got to finish putting your book together. I want the first copy, hot off the press, of *The Legends of Antietam* by Rebecca Knight MacKade."

"That's Dr. MacKade to you," she said and chuckled against his lips. "I'll finish the book very soon now." She turned again, touched a hand to the cool stone that marked a young man's grave. "And we'll finish the rest, together. It's what they wanted from us—John and Sarah."

"I can still feel them. In the house. In the land."

"We always will." Content, Rebecca snuggled into his arms as the wind kicked up and sent snow flying. "But it's different now. Settled."

"Settled." He smiled, resting his cheek on the top of her head. It was a word he'd never expected to apply to himself. But how well it fit, how well she fit. "I love you, Rebecca."

"I know." Still her heart swelled just hearing it. "I love you."

It was the perfect time, she thought. The perfect place. Though she stayed in the circle of his arms, she tilted her head back. She wanted to see his face when she told him, to see what came into his eyes. She drew a breath because the words, the first time they were said, were so precious.

"We're going to have a baby."

His eyes went totally blank, and that made her lips curve. "What?"

How lovely, she thought, to have the chance to say it again. "We're going to have a baby, in a little over eight months." Her smile spread, her eyes filled as she took his limp hand and pressed it to her stomach. "We're going to have a baby," she said a third time.

"You're pregnant." His breath came out in a whoosh, and his eyes were no longer blank. Shock, joy, delight. Everything she'd wanted to see raced into them. "We're pregnant." His gaze dropped down to their joined hands covering a miracle. "Our baby."

"Our baby." Then she let out a rich laugh as she was spun off her feet and into wild circles that sent snow flying into the sunlight.

He stopped as abruptly as he'd begun, and now concern and a touch of fear showed on his face. "You're feeling all right? You're not sick? You don't eat enough. You've got to start eating. Are you sure you feel all right?"

"I feel wonderful. Invincible." She touched her lips to his. "I feel loved."

"Rebecca." His mouth lingered, then gently deepened the kiss, and the arms that cradled her gathered her closer yet. "You are loved." Emotion flowed through him as she nestled her head on his shoulder. His wife. His child. "It's a circle," he murmured, looking down at the stone marker again. "Season to season."

"Yes. If it's a boy, I'd like to name him Cameron."

"It feels right. It all feels so right." He heard his dogs barking in the distance, quick yelps of joy and recognition. "That's the family coming." He kissed her once again, then turned from the snow-draped meadow, boots crunching as he walked back toward the house. "I can't wait to tell them another MacKade's on the way. We need champagne or something. Oh, you can't have any alcohol. Well, we'll come up with something." He glanced down, grinning like a fool. "Hey, that's why you didn't drink anything for New Year's Eve."

"Yes, that's why." She cocked a brow at him. She wondered if he knew he was rambling, and being simply so adorable she wanted to shout with laughter. "Shane, you can put me down now," Rebecca told him.

He only held her closer. "No, I can't."

"You don't have to carry me all the way into the house."

"Yes, I do." His eyes met hers and he laughed. "I've got you now, Rebecca MacKade. I'm not letting go."

* * * * *

Silhouette®

SPECIAL EDITION™

COMING NEXT MONTH

#1027 PART-TIME WIFE—Susan Mallery
That Special Woman!/Hometown Heartbreakers
When Jill Bradford took the position of nanny to three adorable boys, she was determined that it stay a business arrangement. But the boys' father, Craig Haynes, wanted more than just a part-time mother or wife. He wanted Jill forever.

#1028 EXPECTANT FATHER—Leanne Banks
Caleb Masters was intelligent, gorgeous—everything Glory Danson desired in a man. Becoming pregnant with his child, she married for the sake of the baby...but would the expectant father and mom-to-be find love ever after?

#1029 ON MOTHER'S DAY—Andrea Edwards
Great Expectations
When Alex Rinehart reunited Fiona Scott with the daughter she'd given up for adoption, he helped her save the child she thought she'd never see again. And now that Alex and Fiona had found each other, Fiona had more than one reason to celebrate on Mother's Day.

#1030 NEW BRIDE IN TOWN—Amy Frazier
Sweet Hope Weddings
Belle Sherman had arrived and the town of Sweet Hope—and its most eligible bachelor, Boone O'Malley—would never be the same again. When these opposites attracted, there was no stopping Belle from being the next bride in town, unless her groom got cold feet!

#1031 RAINSINGER—Ruth Wind
Daniel Lynch was a drop-dead handsome Navajo with black eyes and an attitude to match. And suddenly Winona Snow found herself sharing her house with him! Soon this stubborn man held the key to her future...and her heart.

#1032 MARRY ME, NOW!—Allison Hayes
She had to save the ranch, but first Dacy Fallon needed to convince old flame Nick Reynolds to accept her help. He wouldn't admit that the old attraction was as strong as ever, but Dacy was determined to win herself a cowboy groom....

MILLION DOLLAR SWEEPSTAKES
AND EXTRA BONUS PRIZE DRAWING

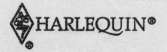

If you are looking for more titles by

NORA ROBERTS

Don't miss this chance to order additional stories by
one of Silhouette's favorite authors:

Silhouette Special Edition®

#09810	§FALLING FOR RACHEL	$3.39	☐
#09872	§CONVINCING ALEX	$3.50	☐
#24000	*THE PRIDE OF JARED MACKADE	$3.75 U.S.	☐
		$4.25 CAN.	☐

§Those Wild Ukrainians miniseries
*The MacKade Brothers

Language of Love

#51040	TREASURES LOST	$3.59	☐
#51039	THE PLAYBOY PRINCE	$3.59	☐
#51038	BLITHE IMAGES	$3.59	☐
#51032	GABRIEL'S ANGEL	$3.59	☐
#51031	ONE SUMMER	$3.59	☐

(limited quantities available on certain titles)

TOTAL AMOUNT	$
POSTAGE & HANDLING	$
($1.00 for one book, 50¢ for each additional)	
APPLICABLE TAXES**	$_____
TOTAL PAYABLE	$_____

(check or money order—please do not send cash)

To order, complete this form and send it, along with a check or money order
for the total above, payable to Silhouette Books, to: In the U.S.: 3010 Walden
Avenue, P.O. Box 9077, Buffalo, NY 14269-9077; In Canada: P.O. Box 636,
Fort Erie, Ontario, L2A 5X3.

Name:_____

Address: _____City:_____

State/Prov.:_____Zip/Postal Code:_____

**New York residents remit applicable sales taxes.
  Canadian residents remit applicable GST and provincial taxes.   SNRBACK6

Silhouette®
TM

"I've been baby-sitting sweet little Lass,

but I'd never let on that I loved her rugged
rancher daddy as much as I do her. Imagine my
surprise when Sam Frazier proposed! Perhaps this
is a marriage of convenience for now, but I can
be a real mother to Lass—and maybe one day soon,
my dream will come true and I'll hear my husband
lovingly whisper my name...."

MOLLY DARLING
by
Laurie Paige
(SE #1021)

In April, Silhouette Special Edition brings you

THAT'S MY BABY!

Sometimes bringing up baby can bring surprises...
and showers of love.

As seen on TV!
Free Gift Offer

With a Free Gift proof-of-purchase from any Silhouette® book,
you can receive a beautiful cubic zirconia pendant.

This gorgeous marquise-shaped stone is a genuine cubic
zirconia—accented by an 18" gold tone necklace.
(Approximate retail value $19.95)

Send for yours today...
compliments of ▼ *Silhouette*®
™

To receive your free gift, a cubic zirconia pendant, send us one original proof-of-
purchase, photocopies not accepted, from the back of any Silhouette Romance™,
Silhouette Desire®, Silhouette Special Edition®, Silhouette Intimate Moments®
or Silhouette Shadows™ title available in February, March or April at your favorite
retail outlet, together with the Free Gift Certificate, plus a check or money order for
$1.75 U.S./$2.25 CAN. (do not send cash) to cover postage and handling, payable
to Silhouette Free Gift Offer. We will send you the specified gift. Allow 6 to 8 weeks for
delivery. Offer good until April 30, 1996 or while quantities last. Offer valid in the U.S. and
Canada only.

Free Gift Certificate

Name: _____

Address: _____

City: _____ State/Province: _____ Zip/Postal Code: _____

Mail this certificate, one proof-of-purchase and a check or money order for postage
and handling to: SILHOUETTE FREE GIFT OFFER 1996. In the U.S.: 3010 Walden
Avenue, P.O. Box 9057, Buffalo NY 14269-9057. In Canada: P.O. Box 622, Fort Erie,

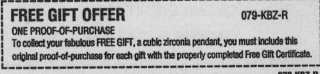

FREE GIFT OFFER   079-KBZ-R
ONE PROOF-OF-PURCHASE
To collect your fabulous FREE GIFT, a cubic zirconia pendant, you must include this
original proof-of-purchase for each gift with the properly completed Free Gift Certificate.

079-KBZ-R

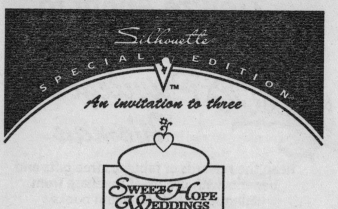

Silhouette

SPECIAL EDITION ™

An invitation to three

Sweet Hope Weddings

from Amy Frazier

Marriages are made in
Sweet Hope, Georgia— where the
newlyweds-to-be are the last to find out!

❤❤❤❤❤

New Bride in Town
(#1030, May '96)

Waiting at the Altar
(#1036, June '96)

A Good Groom Is Hard To Find
(#1043, July '96)

❤❤❤❤❤

Marital bliss is just a kiss away!
Celebrate the joy—only in
Silhouette Special Edition.

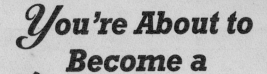

You're About to Become a

Privileged Woman

Reap the rewards of fabulous free gifts and benefits with proofs-of-purchase from Silhouette and Harlequin books

Pages & Privileges™

It's our way of thanking you for buying our books at your favorite retail stores.

PROOF OF PURCHASE
SSE-PP126
Offer expires October 31, 1996

Pages & Privileges ™

™

**Harlequin and Silhouette—
the most privileged readers in the world!**

For more information about Harlequin and Silhouette's PAGES & PRIVILEGES program call the Pages & Privileges Benefits Desk: 1-503-794-2499

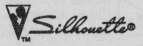

Silhouette®
™